Karen Winters Schwartz

EARLY BIRD

Early Bird
Red Adept Publishing, LLC
104 Bugenfield Court
Garner, NC 27529
https://RedAdeptPublishing.com/
Copyright © 2025 by Karen Winters Schwartz. All rights reserved.

---

1. http://StreetlightGraphics.com

Chapter 1: Baby Birds and Turkeys

Robin heard the baby bird before she saw it. It looked a lot like ET, lying in the grass, its feet pointing to the sky, the skin on its belly nearly see-through. It was fluttering its stubby wings and appeared to be trying to right itself. "A baby bird," she whispered, as she tended to do when something was especially interesting. She bent down and carefully picked it up.

Robin thought about the time when she was nearly four years old and realized she was named after a bird. It was probably her first real memory. She was mad about it. She did not have stick legs that bent in a funny way. She did not have feathers or a beak. What had made her really mad was that she could not fly. She had been nearly five before she realized just how embarrassing her name really was and what a bad sense of humor Mommy and Daddy had. "You need to learn your full name before you start kindergarten next week," said Mommy. "Your name is Robin Aletta Byrd. Can you remember that?"

"My name is Robin A Little Bird?"

It had been a week before she talked to either of them.

Now that she was seven, she was pretty much over being mad. She'd recently learned from Daddy that Aletta meant "winged one" in Spanish, which was kind of nice.

Even though she was learning to like her name, Robin was not particularly fond of birds. It probably had to do with that movie she'd watched when she was only five. Her parents had been out for the evening, and her older brother, Jay, convinced the babysitter that the old movie *The Birds* was something they'd all enjoy. Luckily, her little sister, Wren, who was only three at the time, had fallen asleep pretty much right away. Over two years later, Robin still had nightmares about telephone booths.

But somehow, as she squatted in the grass of her backyard and held the baby bird in her hand, all that changed. Its beak was huge and opened every time she said, "Hi, little bird." Tiny white feathers were sprouting out around its eyes and on the sides of its belly and wings. The tips of the new feathers sparkled in the weak morning sun. The rest of it was covered with soft gray fuzz. She shifted to her knees, feeling wetness from the grass soaking into her jeans and the cool spring air of Central New York hitting her face, and knew the little bird with so few feathers must really be cold. She looked up at the sugar maple that towered over her. There wasn't a nest in sight. She stood up carefully, cradling Sparkle—yes, that was his new name—in both her hands.

"Mommy," she said as she passed through the screen door. It slammed behind her, the spring snapping shut. "Mommy, look what I found." Robin looked up from Sparkle and did a quick scan of the bright-yellow kitchen.

Mommy was leaning into the freezer. Her feet were bare, and she was standing on her toes, as if she were about to crawl right on in.

"There it is," said Mommy, stepping back and smiling at the big frozen turkey she held in her hands. "Dinner! How will I ever get this monster thawed and cooked in time?"

"Mommy, look!" Robin held out the little bird, and as she did, Sparkle opened his mouth, let out a loud whistling noise, and flopped to the floor, his little wings doing nothing to slow his fall. Mommy screamed and dropped the turkey, which fell much faster than Sparkle. It landed right on her foot.

Mommy cried out, using a bad word that no one, not even Daddy, was allowed to use. Robin snatched up Sparkle. He seemed to be okay. Mommy jumped on one foot before sinking to the kitchen floor, tears running down her face. "Oh my God. Oh my God."

"Mommy? Are you okay?" Robin held Sparkle against her chest.

"What the hell is going on in there?" asked Daddy. He appeared at the threshold between the family room and the kitchen. Robin could hear the TV over Mommy's moans. "Lizzie? What happened?" Seconds later, he was by Mommy's side. Her whole foot was growing. Her toes were bent in a funny way—and starting to puff up like pink sausages.

"Jay!" Daddy yelled toward the family room.

"What?" answered Jay, all sleepy and annoyed.

"Dammit, Jay, get in here."

Robin started to cry. Five-year-old Wren walked in, looked around, and started to cry too. Sparkle joined in with his open-mouth whistle. Jay walked in slowly and leaned against the doorjamb. "Geez, what's all the fuss about?"

Robin didn't like him much now that he was thirteen.

Daddy scooped up Mommy as if she were nothing. "You're in charge," Daddy said to Jay.

"What? No way," said Jay. "You can't leave me alone with them."

Daddy headed for the door.

"My purse," Mommy said and pointed.

Daddy swung her near the counter so she could grab the purse.

"Daddy," Robin said through her tears, "what about Sparkle? I found him in the yard."

He stopped momentarily and stared at the little gray bird, which Robin held up for him to see. Sparkle opened his mouth and whistled a chirp. "Throw him back outside. Baby birds and humans just don't mesh. Heartache and tragedy, that's what I'm looking at." He carried Mommy carefully through the screen door. It slammed with a bang. Sparkle flapped his helpless little wings, turned his head up toward Robin, and blinked. His cute white eyelids fluttered closed like he'd seen quite enough for one day.

Author Note: While the human characters in this story and what happens in their lives are strictly created by my imagination, the bird encounters depicted in Early Bird *are all based on true-life events. Like little-girl Robin in the story, I'm not a huge fan of birds. Yet I've been a part of so many cool and amazing bird interactions. Some are funny, some are tragic, but all are poignant and remind me of my place on Earth. I am but one little speck of life in a magical universe of birds, bees, and innumerable creatures of various stature, all of equal importance. P.S. The names of the birds have not been changed to protect the innocent; they are their exact given names when they flew into my life.*

Chapter 2: Hard-Boiled Egg

Robin pressed Sparkle against her chest and wiped at her tears with her free hand. Wren began to wail at the sound of the car starting and the crunch of the gravel as Daddy backed down the driveway.

"Stop crying," said Jay. He batted Wren gently on the head, causing her light-brown ponytail to flip forward onto her face and then back again. Stepping forward, he gave the frozen turkey a little kick with his foot. "I don't even like turkey. Bet we're going to be able to order pizza tonight."

Wren stopped sobbing long enough to say, "I like turkey."

"But you also like pizza," said Jay.

"Jay," said Robin. "What about Sparkle?"

"Sparkle? What the heck are you taking about?"

"My bird. Sparkle."

"Oh. That thing? Throw it back outside like Dad said."

"But Jay." Robin gave him her best sad face ever. Even hard-hearted Jay would melt over this face. After all, she'd practiced it in the mirror just yesterday.

"Birds have lice. Get it the hell out of here."

Only Daddy was allowed to say hell. Robin switched to her I-hate-you face and stomped past him, up the stairs, and into her bedroom. She slammed the door but not so hard that it would scare Sparkle, who looked around with renewed interest at the butterfly-covered walls of her bedroom. "Let's make you a little nest." She emptied the polka-dot box of rubber bands she'd been collecting for her world's largest rubber band ball, shaking the last of the holdouts onto her green shag carpet—she'd picked green because it reminded her of the Great Out-doors, as Daddy liked to call it. She lined the box with her softest socks and panties. Once she had the perfect indentation, she set Sparkle in-side. He seemed happy enough. When she was convinced he couldn't get out on his own, she said, "I'm going to go find you something to eat." Sparkle opened his mouth in what looked like a big yes.

Jay ignored her as she walked past, never looking up from the TV. Wren was crashed out on the couch, breathing deeply, her face still wet from tears. A quick Google search on Mommy's phone, which she'd left plugged into the kitchen outlet, and Robin was all set. All she needed was a hard-boiled egg. Like on Easter. Strange to feed a bird an egg, but that was what Google said, and Google was never wrong. But how ex-actly did one hard-boil an egg? After googling that, Robin decided it seemed simple enough—except she was strictly forbidden from touch-ing the stove.

"I'd like a hard-boiled egg, please," she yelled toward the family room.

"What?"

"I'm hungry. You're in charge. I'd like a hard-boiled egg."

"Yeah. Right. I'll get right on that."

Robin rolled her eyes. Jay used to be nice. She used to love having a big brother. This was definitely an emergency situation if there ever was one. Mommy would understand. Robin carefully followed a YouTube video. She was actually hungry, so she made herself one too. That way she wasn't even lying.

Twenty minutes later, she walked by Jay with two hard-boiled eggs, one carefully chopped up and the second peeled and perfect. "Jerk," she said.

"Whatever," answered Jay.

Next stop was her parents' bathroom, where Robin grabbed the set of tweezers Mommy used to pull hairs from her chin and make her eye-brows shaped like she was always surprised.

As soon as Robin reentered her bedroom and said his name, Sparkle started up with his mouth and the whistle. Turned out it wasn't easy grabbing pieces of hard-boiled egg with tweezers, but before long, Robin had it all figured out. Sparkle seemed to have no issues eating a baby cousin. Robin decided she could be dropping chopped-up pieces of rubber bands in there, and he'd be cool with it. A few minutes later, and he stopped opening his mouth. He looked up at her gratefully, ruffled what feathers he had, shut his eyes, and fell asleep.

"I love you, Sparkle," Robin said and immediately recalled Daddy's words: "Heartache and tragedy, that's what I'm looking at."

Robin leaned against her bed and took a bite out of her egg. Daddy was seldom wrong, but in this case, he just was. He had to be.

*A*uthor Note: *Years ago, when one of my daughters found Sparkle in our driveway, we feed him cut-up worms for that first day until we figured out what kind of bird he was. (More on this in Chapter 3) Feeding worms to a baby bird is a no-no according to Google. But hard-boiled eggs? Seems like worms make a lot more sense!*

Chapter 3: Pizza, It Is

Mommy used both her hands to lift and reposition her foot on the pile of pillows stacked up on the stool. She made a face from the pain and slid down a little lower on the family room couch. Her cast went halfway up her calf and was lime green. Wren had already used markers and decorated it with tons of misshaped hearts.

"Please, hand me another piece of pizza, will you, Robin?" Mommy asked.

Robin picked the piece with the most mushrooms because she knew Mommy loved mushrooms. "And then," Robin continued, placing the piece of pizza on Mommy's plate, "after he ate a bunch more egg an hour later—"

"I don't know how I'm supposed to keep my foot above my head and manage to drink and eat," said Mommy.

"Sparkle chirped what almost sounded like a burp."

"Eggs make me fart," said Jay.

"I'm thinking there might be something better than egg," Robin continued. She was really starting to worry about the little guy.

"Everything makes you fart," said Daddy.

The rest of the family laughed, including Mommy, scrunching up her face again right after. Robin did not join in.

"Don't make me laugh," said Mommy.

"Farts are funny," said Wren. She had pizza sauce smeared over her entire face. There was even a little cheese in her hair, which looked especially gross against her dark curls.

"So, what do you think, Mommy? What else can I feed him?"

"You are, like, obsessed with that bird," said Jay. "It's annoying."

"Jay," said Daddy, "it's nice that your sister wants to try to save it."

"This coming from the guy who wanted to throw the thing back outside," said Jay.

Daddy punched Jay gently on the shoulder.

Jay pretended it was a hard punch, fell off the chair, grabbed his leg, and rolled around on the floor. "My foot! My foot! You broke it."

Daddy and Jay were always goofing around. Robin knew that Daddy was super happy he wasn't the only boy in the family. But now was not the time for goofing around.

"Mommy."

"Not funny," said Mommy to Jay.

Robin was mad. She was mad because no one seemed to love Sparkle the way she did, and she was especially mad because she did really love him, and it was scary to love something so helpless. Daddy's words kept popping into her head. Tragedy. Heartache. If heartache was anything like a stomachache, Robin didn't want anything to do with it.

"Mommy."

"Yeah, Jay, not funny. Too soon," said Daddy. "Too soon."

"Mommy!" Robin stomped her foot a little and almost slammed her hands down on the coffee table. She stopped herself just in time. Mommy hated it when Robin slammed her hands on the table. "Sparkle! I need your help."

"Geez, Robin. Chill," said Jay.

Robin swung her face Jay's way, but Mommy made a warning noise and put up her hand before Robin had a chance to do and say what she really wanted.

"Robin, honey," said Mommy in her calm voice. "First thing we need to do is to try to figure out what kind of bird Sparkle is. Take my phone, run upstairs, and take some pictures of him, okay?"

Robin was halfway up the stairs when she heard Mommy say, "Matt, can you hand me that bottle of pain meds they gave me? And maybe give me a swig of your beer?"

Robin snuggled closer to Mommy as they searched the laptop. Wren sat on the other side, slowly picking cheese out of her hair, her eyes half shut with sleep. Jay had disappeared somewhere, probably to plot his next act of meanness. Mommy scrolled to a new page. There were so many pictures of baby birds.

"There he is!" Robin pointed at the picture of the little gray bird on the screen. She held the picture she had just taken next to the screen. "No, that's not him." She sighed. They'd been at it a good ten minutes.

"This website says baby birds should be put back in the nest," said Mommy.

"I told you I looked."

"And if the nest can't be located, you should tape up a homemade one close to where a baby bird was found."

"No, Mommy. He's happy where he is."

"He's a wild animal," said Daddy from his big leather chair across from the couch. He was reading the paper, and all Robin could see was the front page of the sports section. "He should live a wild life."

Robin felt her eyes fill with tears. "He's happy where he is," she repeated. "He likes my room."

"Let's try a different approach to figure out what he is," said Mommy. She shifted her foot again and let out a tiny moan.

"Sorry about your foot. Sorry I scared you."

Mommy took her hand from the keyboard and gave Robin a small squeeze. "Hey, turkeys happen. It was an accident. Guess that's what I get when I buy a Butterball."

Daddy chuckled. Robin laughed, too, but she didn't really get it.

Mommy typed in a few things and finally found a baby-bird-identification app. After she answered a few questions, images appeared on the screen. They scanned the page. "There he is!" This time Robin was sure.

"A cedar waxwing," said Mommy. She clicked a few things until the most beautiful bird looked back at Robin.

"Sparkle's mama," whispered Robin. She touched the screen gently and ran her finger over the grayish-brown neck and lingered on the yellow belly. "She has a feather hat like a cardinal and a black mask like it's Halloween."

"Look at the red tip on her wings," said Mommy. "And look at this other picture. Here, there's a berry in her mouth."

Daddy put down his newspaper and stepped over to look at the screen. "I've seen those birds in the yard before. Cool."

Robin smiled deep inside. Daddy had said cool. There was no way he'd make her toss Sparkle back to the wild. After a few more minutes of internet research, Robin knew that there would be no more eggs in Sparkle's future, just lots of berries.

Author Note: One of the things I like to write about in my novels is family dynamics. There are so many complicated and interesting families of creatures in the world, humans being one of the most intriguing. The great thing about writing character-driven fiction is that, as the writer, I don't always know at the beginning of a novel who will end up being the driving force of the story. This is the getting-to-know-you stage, which hopefully leads to "getting to like you." Is Jay really as uncaring as he seems? What's the real relationship between Robin's parents? And Wren, what's up with her? Thank you for joining me as we all find out.

Chapter 4: How to Be a Real Bird

Sparkle clutched the collar of Robin's pajamas and nestled deeper into her hair. She could hear him chirping quietly near her left ear. In the last week, he'd learned to perch without wobbling on the tree branch Daddy had brought into her bedroom and flap his little wings as if he knew what was coming. His wing feathers had grown out, and his belly was no longer naked. He had a special call just for Robin. Even though Mommy had told her he was not to sleep in her bed, Robin knew that Mommy couldn't get up the stairs. They were safe for the night.

Robin switched off her bedside lamp, carefully lowered herself deeper under the covers, and closed her eyes as Sparkle repositioned himself. "Sweet dreams, my love. And please, try not to poop as much as you did last night."

There was a soft knock on her door. Robin's eyes flew open. Had Mommy somehow gotten up the stairs? The door opened. Light from the hallway sliced across her green shag carpet and landed in her eyes.

"Hey, Worm," Daddy said as he made his way into the room. Robin loved when Daddy called her Worm, especially now that it seemed to be happening less and less. "Can I turn the light back on?"

Robin nodded. Daddy stepped up to the bed, reached for the lamp switch, and sat on the edge of the bed. He glanced toward Sparkle's branch. "Where's the little guy?"

Robin shrugged because she didn't want to say an outright lie. Sparkle shifted with the movement and gave out a pretty loud "Is it time to feed me again?" whistle.

"Don't know where he is, huh?"

"Nope," she said with a smile.

Daddy did a little eyeroll, the kind that Mommy really hated. Then he put his hand on her knee and said, "Listen, Worm, Sparkle is growing up fast. We have to talk about his future."

"His future? Like you talk to Jay about what college he might go to?"

"Funny. Let me rephrase. Birds are amazing creatures because they can do what so many animals can't. They can soar high above the rest of us. How wonderfully free that must feel, don't you think?"

She nodded. Robin dreamed about flying all the time. In her dreams, she flew over everything and everybody she knew. No one ever bothered to look up and see her. It was wonderful.

"I think we need to give Sparkle a chance at being a real bird, don't you?"

"I guess so."

"I think he needs to go back outside to learn about the big, wild world. He needs to learn to be a bird."

"But he's still little. He can't quite fly. What about Mrs. Markingson's cat, Seymour?"

"Don't you worry. I have a plan." Daddy had a lot of plans. Most of them were good. After all, he was an engineer and worked at doing important things. "Tomorrow is Saturday. We'll set my plan into motion right after breakfast." He switched off the light, kissed Robin's head, and lightly patted her long dark curls right near where Sparkle was hiding. "Good night, Sparkle." He stood up, tiptoed in an exaggerated way, and right before he shut her door with the softest of clicks, he said, "I won't tell your mom."

It took Robin a while to fall asleep. How could Sparkle learn about the big, wild world and still be safe? If only she could learn how to soar too. Then she could always protect him. She crossed her fingers really hard and hoped like crazy she'd dream about flying.

Mommy and Daddy used to have a dog. His name had been Finch, and he died before Jay was born. He was brown and fuzzy and looked a lot like a dirty mop. His three pictures were bigger than the ones of Jay, Robin, and Wren and placed smack in the middle of the mantel. The one Robin liked best showed Mommy on one side of him and Daddy on the other. They looked so young and carefree, making Robin wonder at times if they'd be happier if the three of them were dogs.

Maybe they always planned to get another dog, because from way up in the attic—which was a very scary place—Daddy dragged down an old collapsible wire kennel they'd used when Finch was a puppy. He set it up on the front deck, facing the woods on the side of their property so that Sparkle would have a view. "You see, he'll get fresh air and be able to practice flying, but cats and other predators won't be able to get through the bars."

"But Sparkle can get through," said Robin as she handed Daddy another branch—this one with lots of fresh leaves to give Sparkle shade and make him feel safe.

Wren walked onto the deck, carrying a big pile of old wet leaves and twigs.

"It's just as if he were in a nest," said Daddy. "That's the freedom part. The being a wild bird part." Daddy wedged the branches between the bars of the kennel, weaving them together until they started looking like the inside of a real tree. Wren shoved leaf after muddy leaf into the cage, dirt and little twigs falling onto the deck. A few worms fell free from the leaves, confused, with nowhere to go.

"But that's what got him in trouble in the first place." Robin bit her lower lip and tried not to cry. She picked up the misplaced worms and a few stray bugs, throwing them off the deck and onto the grass, where they'd be happier.

"We talked about this, remember? You can still feed him. Make sure he has water."

Robin nodded, but she wasn't sure that the freedom part was all it was cracked up to be.

"Okay," said Daddy. "I think we're about set. Go get the little dude, and let's see how he likes his new home."

Robin walked toward the stairs like she was walking toward death. Mommy was sleeping on her spot on the couch, her foot propped up, old cups and dishes surrounding her. Her bottle of pain meds was left open on the coffee table along with an old glass of white wine made dark with dead fruit flies. Robin hoped the pain pills wouldn't make Mommy so out of it that she woke up and drank it without looking first.

Sparkle chirped happily the whole way downstairs, through the house, and out the back door. His head popped up in what looked like wonder and surprise at the sight of the big wild world. Maybe he'd forgotten all about it in the last ten days. She placed him carefully in the center of the tree in the cage that Daddy had made. Sparkle grabbed on immediately, flapped his wings a few times, bobbed up and down, and whistled his feed-me-please song. Robin was ready with raspberries, which were his favorite. Wren and she took turns popping berry after berry into his sweet little mouth until he closed his eyes, ruffled his feathers, and fell asleep.

"He seems content to me," said Daddy.

And as much as Robin wanted to disagree, she just couldn't.

Author Note: While they do eat insects, Cedar Waxwings love fruit and live almost exclusively on berries in the summer months. Our neighbors across the road from us in Central New York had rows of wonderful raspberries. We're sure that's why Sparkle's parents picked our yard to have their babies. These berry-loving birds are actually little winos, of-

ten eating so much overripe and fermenting fruit that they get inebriated, fluttering about, crashing into windows, and wobbling on their branches.

Chapter 5: Mamas and Babies

Robin pushed the slice of hotdog around on her plate, making a little moat through the baked beans. She wasn't very hungry, and it was the third time since Mommy's foot was broken that they'd had franks and beans.

Mommy sat across from Daddy, pushing her hotdogs around too.

Daddy had made Mommy come to the table. "It's been over a week now, Lizzie. It's time to join the living."

The only thing she seemed to be putting into her mouth was her wine. Not the wine full of fruit flies but a new glass, which started out filled clear to the top, and this time the wine was deep red. Her foot was resting on a spare chair. Her toes peeking out from the cast were still purple and fat.

"I'm worried about Sparkle out there all alone tonight," said Robin. "Maybe I should just bring him in for the night."

"No," said Daddy.

Daddy wasn't in a very good mood.

"I'll put him right back out in the morning."

"Your father said no, Robin." Mommy took a long drink from her glass. "Matt, can you go get the bottle of wine from the counter?"

Robin knew Daddy wanted to say no to that too. They all watched as he struggled with Mommy's request.

"I'll get it," said Wren, jumping up from the table and skipping the three steps to the counter.

"Really, Lizzie? You're having your children fetch your booze now?"

"Oh, I don't mind," said Wren, skipping back to Mommy. She seemed totally clueless to how mad Daddy was. "It smells like old raspberries." Wren pushed her face to the top of the bottle, getting a ring of wine on the tip of her nose.

"Booze? Really, Matt? Booze? It's a glass of wine, not whiskey."

"Ethanol is ethanol," said Daddy. "Chemistry 101."

"Guess there's a reason why they call alcoholics winos, right, Dad?" said Jay.

Robin knew if Mommy could, she would stomp out of the room. And because she couldn't, she began to cry.

Even Wren was beginning to realize something was up and stopped, letting her hand holding the wine bottle drop to her side. "Mommy?"

Mommy put her arms out to Wren, and Wren flew inside them. "It's okay, honey. Mommy is okay. It's just that my foot really hurts." She shot Daddy a look, asking him to understand, but he wiped his mouth with his napkin, and he used his eyes to show he didn't.

Robin wanted to do something to make it better. She almost brought up Sparkle again. Instead, she ate her beans really fast and said, "This is so good! Do you think we can have this every night?"

"I love franks and beans," said Jay. "Cowboys eat beans every night. I think most of them would be thrilled to have a dog thrown in there."

It was not that many years ago that Jay had been obsessed with cowboys. There were tons of pictures from when he was little, wearing a hat, chaps, gun holster—the entire cowboy getup. He used to talk endlessly about how he was going to move to the West and work at a real cattle ranch. Robin hadn't heard him talk about it in ages. Of course, he barely talked these days. It made Robin happy deep inside to know that he still had a little cowboy in him.

She smiled at him and said, "How about a rattlesnake? Do you think they eat those?"

He nodded, working on chewing what was in his mouth, before he said, "Roast 'em on a spit over the fire, saving the skin and rattle for a belt. Bet I could shoot a rattlesnake right between the eyes."

"Poor snake," said Mommy as she carefully removed Wren from her body and took the bottle of wine. She filled up her glass, clear to the brim, and raised an eyebrow at Daddy. He glared at her.

"Daddy," said Robin.

"Daddy," she said again.

He finally turned his eyes her way.

"Did you ever shoot anything?"

"I'm an engineer," said Daddy. "Engineers don't need guns. We out-think our enemies."

Mommy made a little noise.

Robin pushed on. "I bet if you did ever have to shoot something, you'd be really good at it. You're good at everything. Just like Mommy is."

"Don't be so lame," said Jay. Just like that, he was right back to his new self.

Robin wanted to cry like Wren had. Instead, she said, "Can I be excused? I want to go check on Sparkle."

"Sure," said Daddy. "But take your plate to the sink."

The sun was low in the sky, just starting to get big and fuzzy. It was almost to the point that Robin could look at it without her eyes snapping shut in protest. The air smelled like flowers, which was so much better than the smell of franks and beans that seemed to have settled into the house since Mommy's foot got hurt. Robin took in a big breath of fresh air and let it out slowly. Birds were chirping their evening songs, the ones that meant they were getting ready for bed. She felt a little bit of happiness start to grow as she took another deep breath. The big wild world really was something.

Sparkle must have heard the screen door snap shut, because as she stepped to the side of the house and onto the deck, she could hear him whistling away. She realized as she got closer that she'd forgotten to bring his dinner. The tiny bit of happiness disappeared, because she really didn't want to go back in there just now. She sighed and was about to turn around when a strange movement caught her eye. Was something else in the cage with Sparkle? Her heart jumped in her chest. Was it a rat? Would a rat eat a bird? Before she could react, the "rat" took flight, easily slipping between the metal bars, and flew to the nearest tree.

Robin ran closer. It was a bird. A beautiful mama bird that looked just like the picture on the laptop. Sparkle chirped from the kennel, and Mama Bird called back.

Another bird joined in and then swooped toward Robin's head. Daddy Bird. His chirp wasn't so friendly. He landed on a branch above Mama Bird's head and fussed at Robin. "Go away! Go away!" he seemed to be saying. He dove at her again.

"Mommy! Daddy!" Robin yelled. "Come see! Come see! Sparkle found his family!" She ran back around the house, the screen door slamming behind her.

"Whoa there," said Daddy. "You almost knocked over the chair."

"Come see! Come see!" Robin tugged at Daddy's arm. "All of you. You have to come see!"

By the time they all got out there, Mama Bird was back in the kennel. She dropped the berry she was about to give Sparkle and flew back to the tree.

"Did you see? Sparkle found his family!" She pointed at the tree. "See? There's his daddy too!"

"Well, would you look at that. And after all this time," said Mommy.

"He's going to be a real bird, just like you said, Daddy."

Sparkle bobbed up and down on his branch and whistled.

Daddy put his right arm around Robin and used his other arm to help steady Mommy on her crutches. Mommy leaned in and rested her head on Daddy's shoulder. Wren wrapped herself around Mommy's good leg, and even Jay stepped forward and placed his hand on Robin's back.

"Cool," he said.

And they all stood extra still until Mama Bird flew back to the kennel, picked up the fallen berry, and dropped it into her baby's open, waiting mouth.

*A*uthor Note: *The mama and daddy cedar waxwings fed the real Sparkle day after day, flying right through the bars of the dog kennel. At some point, Sparkle must have decided it was time to leave the safety of his enclosure. For a few days, we saw his parents taking care of him in the yard before they all disappeared. I'd like to say he came back once in a while for a little visit, pecked at our windowpanes, and landed on our fingers, but we never saw him again. Or if we did, we didn't recognize him in his grown-up state. The people across the road got older and died. Their raspberry bushes weren't far behind, and the cedar waxwings flew on to "berrier" pastures.*

Chapter 6: Eggs and Angels

Robin specifically remembered going to bed on her eighth birthday and realizing she'd gone through the entire day without crying for the first time in her life. Mom had just returned from the retreat she'd gone to not long after her cast was removed. It was nice to have her back. She'd been gone forever and was home just in time for Robin's birthday. Jay said it was a place for drunks. Dad said it was a retreat, which sounded so much better—so that was what Robin and Wren called it.

Robin had decided growing up was all about not crying, and she was very eager to grow up, so she had not cried in three years. In third grade, Michelle Newburg had told everyone in school that Robin had bird mites, but Robin never cried. At ten years old, when Robin had sprained her wrist after falling out of a tree, she bit her lip and forced back tears. Later that year, when Mom had accidentally started to drive off before Robin got fully in the car, Mom cried and cried, but Robin never cried once, even though her big toe grew as big as a golf ball.

But after opening the final wrapped gift on her eleventh birthday—just a turquoise blouse—Robin felt tears well up in her eyes. Mom just smiled, jumped up from the kitchen table, and said it was time to cut the cake.

All Robin wanted for her birthday was an incubator and quail eggs. She had made it abundantly clear. She'd been pretty much obsessed with bobwhite quails ever since she read *That Quail, Robert*, by Margaret A. Stanger, even though the book was nearly fifty years old. And her family had given her nothing but clothes. Even Wren had given her a pair of socks. Sure, they had birds on them, but still. Jay hadn't been able to get home from Boston University, and all he'd sent her was an emoji of a cake followed by one of a bird.

"Is something wrong?" asked Dad.

He'd been away a lot, traveling for work, and Robin knew he'd made a special effort to be here. She sucked in a breath and willed herself not to cry.

"Close your eyes, honey, while I light the candles."

"Lizzie, hang on," said Dad. "Do you hear something?"

Mom stopped what she was doing, cocked her head, and asked, "Is that coming from the garage?"

Robin listened and didn't hear a thing other than the hum of the refrigerator and the heater blowing hot air out the floor vents of the old house. It was an unusually cold and dreary November. "It's the heater," she said.

Wren began to laugh. "It's not a heater. It's a surprise!" she yelled.

Dad rolled his eyes. "Our little secret keeper."

"Wait. What? My eggs?" Robin jumped from the table and ran to the door that led to the garage. Cold air hit her face as she stepped into the garage. On the hood of Dad's car sat a box with a picture of a yellow-topped incubator. Next to it was a smaller box. "My eggs," she whispered. She picked the box up gently and looked at her parents. "My eggs?"

Mom nodded, smiling from ear to ear. "A dozen."

"We are supposed to keep them cold, so I figured we'd hide them in the garage," said Dad.

"Daddy must have heard cheeping from inside the eggs," said Wren.

"They have to be incubated, Wren," said Robin. "Right, Dad? That's why they're still cold." She had just started calling him Dad, and it still felt odd.

"That's right." He put a hand on Wren's head and said, "We were just joking about hearing something out here."

"Like a monster."

Wren was always worrying about monsters and lots of other things. It seemed like at nearly nine years old, she'd be over the monster stage. Robin knew Mom still had to check under her bed and in her closet every night before Wren would go to sleep. It made Robin a little worried. She had messaged Jay on Mom's laptop just a few days ago: *Do you think there's something wrong with Wren? Mom took her to some new specialist.*

Naw was all he'd typed back and never answered her follow-up questions. Not even an emoji. She'd deleted the conversation so Mom wouldn't see it. The last thing she wanted to do was to make Mom more stressed. But today Mom was having a good day, and she beamed as she watched Robin pick up the smaller of the two boxes off the car.

Robin opened the box carefully and pulled aside the paper wrapping inside until she found the miniature egg carton. She held her breath and lifted the lid, revealing twelve tiny cream-colored eggs with brown speckles. Her heart went all aflutter. They were the loveliest eggs she'd ever seen.

That night, Robin lay on her side with her head on her pillow and stared at the little eggs through the plastic lid of the incubator, which sat on her nightstand. It had taken less than an hour to read the instructions and set it up. It had special pegs that automatically turned the eggs every few hours and built-in water channels to control the humidity. Dad had for sure done his research.

In about twenty-one days, she'd have twelve beautiful baby quails. She couldn't wait to get to school the next day and tell everyone about her eggs. Except maybe Michelle Newburg. Of all the annoying girls in her class, Michelle was the worst. Always brushing her hair and flirting with the boys like she was a teenager already or something. Sure, she was the only one of them who had started to look like a teenager, but that didn't make her special or anything. It just made her a freak. Not that Robin was still bitter about the bird-mite thing. She was over it, but Michelle would never be one of her peeps.

There was a knock on her bedroom door.

"Come in," she called. She knew it was Wren because only Wren knocked on her door like a butterfly might—a fluttering of fingers so slight that it was almost not there.

"Robin," Wren whispered as she stepped into the room. "Can I say good night to the eggs?"

Her face was so round and so soft, encircled by curls, that Robin sucked in a breath. Angelic was the word that popped into Robin's head. It had been on their vocabulary list just last month. But angels reminded Robin of death, so she pushed that thought out of her head and motioned for Wren to join her in the bed.

They lay there a few moments, peering at the eggs, Wren's back spooned into Robin, before Wren said, "Mommy and Daddy are whisper-fighting again."

Robin hugged her closer. Wren's bedroom was right next to their parents'.

"I think it's about me."

"Naw," Robin said, trying out Jay's word. "Just normal husband-and-wife stuff." It wasn't long before they both fell asleep.

For eight more nights, Robin and Wren lay side by side before falling asleep and watched the twelve little eggs as if they were magic. Night after night, they slept and waited, until the unthinkable happened.

Author Note: The following few chapters are a fictionalized account of when I was a child and my parents let me order a little yellow incubator with a clear dome and six quail eggs that I saw advertised in the back of a children's magazine. I don't remember the name of the magazine,

but the quail eggs turned out a lot better than those Sea Monkeys I also ordered. Back then, incubators didn't come with automatic egg-turning capabilities, and I remember it was a big deal to turn them every few hours. As with all these bird stories, this account is based on what really happened.

Chapter 7: Ice & Fire

Robin woke up to Wren shivering beside her and the sound of the wind pushing itself around the sides of the house. The shutters banged against the siding, which Dad had been meaning to paint for two years now. Their rusty hinges squeaked and groaned like one of Wren's monsters. A branch from the maple tree scraped repeatedly on the roof above her bedroom, reminding Robin of skeleton fingers. Robin was glad her little sister was still asleep. Hard rain, which was more like ice, pelted the bedroom window. The sun was just starting to lighten the sky, which was dark gray.

As if a switch had been flipped, the rain turned from ice to huge flakes of snow. The wind eased back, and the house grew silent. The fluttering fairies outside her window were quiet too. Everything was still.

"Oh, Wren," she whispered. "You should wake up. Our first snow. It's so beautiful." She eased out of bed and tiptoed to the window. It was already starting to stick to the ground. Visions of the snowman she'd build were forming in her head. The clouds of her own breath blurred her view. The house was so cold, so calm, like it, too, was sleeping.

"Oh no!" she cried, making Wren jump. Robin ran to her bedside lamp and switched it on. Nothing happened. She tried the overhead light with the same results.

"What's wrong?" asked Wren, rubbing her eyes and pulling the covers tighter around her.

"The electricity is out."

Robin went to her eggs and squinted in the dim light, trying to read the thermometer within the incubation chamber. She couldn't see the numbers. She opened the chamber as little as possible and withdrew the thermometer, bringing it to the window to get a little better light. Seventy-two, it read.

"Mom! Dad! My eggs!" she yelled, running to the hallway and flinging open their bedroom door. "My eggs!"

The sleeping forms of her parents vaulted into life. Mom nearly fell off her side of the bed.

"They're cold. The electricity is out, and they're cold."

"Whoa. Wait. What?" asked Dad.

She couldn't get enough air into her lungs to say it all again, so she pointed and sucked in breath and gestured for them to come. Mom put the covers over her head, and Dad padded after her.

"What are you doing here?" Dad asked Wren when he saw her wrapped up tight in Robin's bedding.

"Nothing."

"Cold" was all Robin was able to get out. She switched on and off the light switch and pointed at the incubator.

Confusion left his face. "Ah." He rubbed his eyes. "I suppose sitting on them isn't an option."

Some of the panic was starting to leave her. She almost managed a smile, thinking about how gently she'd have to sit down.

"Plus, I have to go to work, and you have to go to school." He again rubbed his eyes and then moved to his hair. "I think I know something simple that might just work."

Robin sat at the kitchen table with Wren. They were both wrapped in extra sweaters, eating cold cereal and staring at the flickering candles. Robin really didn't want to go to school. Not that she didn't trust Mom to monitor the incubator temperature. It was just that when you really cared about something, it was best to do it yourself. She was torn. If the electricity came back on, the crisis would be nearly over. If it didn't, school was sure to be canceled, and she could stay home and stare at the eggs all day.

Dad had set the incubator up on a block made up of a couple of short pieces of scrap two-by-fours and then surrounded it with candles of varying heights. The whole thing glowed like a halo. The thermometer now read ninety-nine. She just had to make sure it didn't get much higher. Or lower. Every once in a while, she reached out and adjusted the position of a candle.

Mom walked into the room, looking like maybe she should go back to bed. She rubbed her face and said, "They just sent a notice that schools are closed." She set her cell phone down on the counter and reached for a coffee cup. "I'm sure glad we have a gas stovetop." She re-lit the tea kettle and spooned instant coffee into her cup. "How are the eggs doing?"

"Ninety-nine!" said Wren, who had milk dripping down her chin and onto the kitchen table.

"That's good, right?"

Robin nodded. The kettle burst into song, as it was still hot from when Dad had used it before he'd left for work.

"Electricity is out throughout most of Syracuse," said Mom as she poured steaming water into her cup and sat down at the kitchen table.

The three of them stared at the little eggs and the dancing flames.

After a few minutes, Mom reached out and covered Robin's hand with her own. "It's going to be okay, honey. You wait and see. Those little babies in there are just fine."

*A*uthor Note: *The ability of birds to apparently sit patiently on their eggs for weeks is impressive. Incubating eggs in a little electronic contraption is not all that easy, and neither is the waiting. Mother Nature*

seems to have it pretty well figured out. Sometimes it's best just to leave it to the universe.

Chapter 8: Twenty-One Days and Counting

The night before the twenty-first day of incubation, Robin barely slept. Luckily, the following day was Sunday, so she would be there when it happened.

The night before the twenty-second day of incubation, Robin didn't sleep at all. She fretted that it would happen while she was at school the next day.

The night before the twenty-third day of incubation, Robin spent most of the night pacing around her room or picking up each of the eggs, putting them next to her ear, or putting them up against the light bulb of the bedside lamp to try to see through the shell. She couldn't hear or see anything. At some point, she must have fallen asleep, because she woke up to Mom knocking on her door.

"Time to get up. You're going to be late for school."

That day at school, she avoided talking to any of her friends in fear that they would ask her about the eggs. She felt the sadness hovering over her. The only thing keeping her from complete despair was hope. She knew the incubation period was anywhere from twenty to twenty-three days, depending on conditions. There was still hope, wasn't there?

Robin stepped off the bus and started to walk toward the house that afternoon, a mixture of dread and cautious optimism slowing her progress. Wren tried to take her hand as they stepped off the sidewalk and onto their driveway, but Robin was afraid she might cry if she felt the softness of Wren's little fingers in hers.

Mom opened the front door as if she'd been poised to do so. She waved her hand—her smile bright and excited. "Go look."

"Really?" Robin broke into a run and took the stairs to the bedroom two at a time.

"He's been working away all day long," Mom said as they all entered the bedroom.

One of the beautiful eggs had a line of chips going around nearly the full circumference.

"Nothing's happened for a while, though. I guess he's resting," Mom continued.

"Only one?" whispered Robin, her face pressed against the incubator.

"Yes. So far."

They watched in silence. The egg and the little bird inside were perfectly still.

"Do you think he's okay?"

"The internet said it was normal for them to rest."

It made Robin happy that Mom had checked on the eggs all day and that she'd cared enough to google about hatching. Robin leaned against her. Mom put her arm around her. Wren leaned in, and they all watched—their breaths fogging up the plastic top.

"It kind of looks like it's drying up," said Wren.

Robin wanted to be mad at her and to tell her that she was wrong.

"I've been spraying the egg with water," said Mom.

"He needs help," whispered Robin.

The three of them stared at the little egg, until Mom said finally, "Then let's help."

Mom left the room and returned shortly with her tweezers—the same ones Robin had used to feed Sparkle all those years ago. "The internet said to just go slowly, and if we see any blood, we're to stop immediately."

"You googled that too?" asked Robin.

"I did." Mom chewed gently on her bottom lip as she picked up the egg and carefully worked at chipping away at what the little bird had already accomplished. Robin imagined blood spurting everywhere. It seemed to take forever. Finally, enough of the eggshell fell away that Robin could see the brown-and-tan down of the baby bird and a small movement as it breathed.

"He's alive." Robin said the words so quietly that she was surprised when Wren nodded in agreement.

Another minute later, the chick made a movement, and he was free of the entire eggshell. He lay there, breathing hard, his downy feathers slightly matted but totally dry, both his legs splayed out. He was dark brown with pretty tan stripes on his face and body. He looked so tired and relieved.

"He really needed help," said Robin. She hugged Mom. "Thank you."

By the time Dad got home from work, little Quentin—which was the perfect name for a quail about the size of a big bumblebee—was up and alert, pecking at his food and drinking water. Dad had made a wooden box equipped with a heat lamp, a stuffed toy goose for snuggling, and food and water at the opposite end. Quentin's down was now fluffed out and felt like silk. He was an absolutely perfect little chick except for one thing. His right leg was still turned out in a funny way, making it difficult for him to get it under him and walk normally.

"I'll call Dick," said Dad as he watched the little quail struggle with his leg.

Mom shook her head and went downstairs to start dinner. Dad was always calling Dr. Stewart for one reason or another. Dr. Stewart was an orthopedic surgeon who lived across the street. Jay said Dad had a man crush on him. Robin didn't quite understand what a man crush was, but Dad always laughed and seemed super happy when Dr. Stewart was around.

"Fourteen years of education, and here I am treating a goddamned bird," said Dr. Stewart as he slowly and gently pulled Quentin's leg one way and then the other.

Dad laughed.

Mom hadn't bothered to come back up and watch the examination.

Quentin looked especially tiny in the doctor's hand. The bird wasn't the least bit concerned. He gently pecked at his fingers and peeped happily. He didn't even seem to notice the smell of cigarette smoke that had settled into the room.

Dr. Stewart put Quentin back into the box, stood up, and reached for the tall glass of brown liquid with ice that he'd brought with him from his house. He swirled it around and took a long drink. Whatever kind of drink it was smelled like old wood. Robin couldn't imagine it tasted very good.

The doctor watched Quentin flop around for a moment and said, "Go get me a little Band-Aid."

Robin jumped at the command, feeling how one of his nurses must feel, and ran into the bathroom. She picked three different sizes of bandages just to be safe. The truth was that she was a little afraid of Dr. Stewart.

He discarded the larger ones by throwing them to the floor and chose the tiniest one. He took another drink from his glass, put it back down, and picked up Quentin. "Unwrap that for me," he said, handing the bandage to Robin.

Her hands were slightly shaky, but she managed to get the wrapper off.

Dr. Stewart bent Quentin's leg so that it was tucked under him and held out his hand to her. As she started to put the bandage between his fingers, he waved his hand impatiently. "Take the entire wrapper off."

Robin decided she would never be a nurse. She glanced up at Dad, but he was only smiling, not noticing or maybe not caring about Dr. Stewart's bossiness. She carefully removed the tabs from both ends of the bandage.

"There you go," he said as he took the fully unwrapped Band-Aid and secured the tiny leg. "I think it's a tendon issue. Putting the leg in the proper position should help."

They watched Quentin hobble around his box on his new little crutch. Already he was moving better.

"Thank you," said Robin.

"Don't thank me too quickly. Wait until you get my bill."

Dad laughed so loudly it kind of hurt Robin's ears.

Dr. Stewart slapped Dad on the shoulder. "Come over for a little drink?"

"Sure thing, Dick."

"Keep it on for a day or so," the doctor said to Robin. "We'll see how it does."

He and Dad left the room.

The ice in his glass tinkled as they walked down the stairs. "A god-damned bird the size of a fucking walnut" was the last thing she heard him say.

Author Note: The scene with the doctor was fun to write. I clearly remember my dad's friend examining my little quail. I was just old enough to understand the nuances of adults. It was my first experience with an orthopedic surgeon. I have had many more over the years, and let me tell you, they are a particular breed among doctors.

Chapter 9: Googly Eyes

None of the other eggs hatched. Robin wanted to break them open and find out at what point in development the baby birds had died, but she was too afraid of what she might see—or smell. She and Wren eventually buried them in the backyard near Finch's gravestone. Wren cried—a lot. Robin was true to her declaration, not shedding a tear.

After four days, Robin was able to remove Quentin's crutch without his leg splaying back out. In less than a week, he was chasing imaginary bugs in the carpet and flapping his little wings, which were already sprouting flight feathers. Robin worried that he was lonely for other birds, because he followed her everywhere, running as fast as he could on his huge pink feet, and he peeped constantly—even when he appeared to be sleeping. It wasn't long before she learned the subtle differences in his calls. He had an *I love you* peep, an *I'm hungry* peep, and an *I'm going to get you* peep that he said to the imaginary bugs. His loudest was his *Don't leave me alone* peep that nearly broke Robin's heart.

In spite of what Google said about the lifespans of quails, Robin had fantasies about packing up Quentin and bringing him with her to college. She'd study ornithology, of course, probably at Cornell. He'd sit on her shoulder during lectures, turning his head back and forth, his beautiful black eyes following the professor's every move.

Quentin grew so fast that by Thanksgiving he was housed in the biggest box they had. It was the box that Mom's new microwave had come in. Her parents wouldn't let Quentin sleep in Robin's bedroom. Mom was still bugged by those sheets she'd had to throw out when

Sparkle was a baby. Instead, his box was set up in the utility room off the kitchen. It wasn't ideal, in Robin's opinion, but she'd given up complaining. As it was, he was almost always with her when she wasn't at school, and she had five days off for Thanksgiving break. She and Quentin had lots of plans.

Mom was flitting about in the kitchen, all keyed up because Jay was coming home for the first time since he'd started college. She was making all his favorite foods, including franks and beans. They were having that tonight, two days before Thanksgiving, and Robin was dreading it. Already, the smell was bringing up unhappy memories. When Mom was away at her retreat, Dad had once again proved he was a better problem solver than a chef. He had bought cans of baked beans the size of bathroom trashcans and bulk cases of hot dogs from Costco, as if Mom were never going to return.

"Frankly," Robin had told him one night, "I never want to eat these again in my life."

Always one to enjoy a good pun, Dad had laughed accordingly, but the following night had been more franks and beans.

It was nice to see Mom so happy, though, and Robin was excited too. She'd missed Jay, with his sulky looks, the way he shuffled through the house, the way he flipped Wren's ponytail, making it spin, and how every once in a while, he put down his cellphone and listened to Robin. But she was also nervous. Jay could be twice as mean as he could be nice.

She and Wren were at the kitchen table, cutting out feathers from different colors of felt and gluing them onto pine cones to make little turkeys with twisted brown pipe-cleaner heads, huge red felt wattles, and plastic googly eyes. Wren had more feathers and scraps of felt stuck on her than she was managing to get on any pine cone. She even had a googly eye stuck onto her right elbow, which made it look like a pirate every time she bent her arm.

Quentin, who was not allowed on the kitchen table, had finally given up trying and jumped from Robin's lap to her feet. Every time one of them dropped something from the table, Quentin chirped with delight and ran over to investigate. Right now, he was dragging a purple turkey feather around like a treasure. He was the funniest little creature Robin had ever known. What she loved the most about him was how excited he was about everything. If she hadn't already decided he was a boy, she'd change his name to Joy.

"Let's see," Mom said. She put her finger to her bottom lip and looked around the room. "What else?"

Wren followed Mom's gaze, as if there was really something to see, but Robin put her head back down and concentrated on the task at hand, trying to decide if the turkey warranted one more yellow feather.

"Popcorn!" Mom yelled, making Robin drop the feather. It sailed to the floor, and Quentin immediately gave up on the purple in favor of the yellow. "I totally forgot to buy popcorn." She slapped herself on the forehead. "Dammit. Dammit."

Robin hunched farther and tried not to see Wren's trembling lip.

"Hey, Wren," Robin said. "What do you think? Do I need another yellow feather?"

"What am I going to do?" asked Mom. "Dammit."

Like an answer to some unsaid prayer, Robin heard the garage door open and the noise from Dad's car as he pulled in.

"He's here!" said Wren. She jumped up from the table. Raining a rainbow of felt, she ran toward the door that led to the garage.

That was apparently more than Quentin could handle, as he dropped the yellow feather and scurried back to Robin's feet.

Mom clapped her hands and followed Wren.

Robin gathered Quentin and placed him on the kitchen table. "Do you like my turkey?" she asked him.

He responded by pulling off the turkey's head and running in tiny circles with it. Decapitated—that was a word and a concept that Robin found fascinating.

She listened to the welcoming ruckus behind her for a moment before picking up Quentin and heading in that direction. Jay walked in from the garage, Wren hanging from his waist like a monkey. He dragged her along without any noticeable effort. How could he be so much taller and older looking in just a few short months? He smiled Robin's way, his teeth a quick flash of white, his eyes sparkling with true pleasure. He was grown up and beautiful. Was this what falling in love was like? Even if it was her own brother?

She held Quentin tight to her chest with one hand and took Jay in with the other. As they hugged, all her fears melted away. He was a savior and sure to fix it all.

Jay pulled away, tapped Quentin on his head, and said, "What a cute little guy."

Author Note: Relationships with siblings are quite complex. I wonder if only children have it easier. Or does the subtle and not-so-subtle dance you do with your siblings vying for parental love, competing for each other's love if there are more than two siblings, and fighting for your own identity prepare you better for adulthood? I was a middle child. I've heard that middle children are especially messed up. All I can tell you is that I always had to sit in the middle of the backseat of the car, and I'm sorry, but that never seemed fair.

Chapter 10: Heartache and Tragedy

Friday after Thanksgiving was always a day when no one went any-where. No Black Friday madness. No movie theater outing. No going out for Chinese food. And this year was to be no different. Dad had even convinced Mom that she didn't need to run to the store for popcorn.

Jay sat at the kitchen table, eating the biggest turkey sandwich Robin had ever seen. It was impressive how wide he could open his mouth. Thick slices of turkey, Durkee Famous Sauce, gobs of cranberry dressing, and even stuffing threatened to spill off the sides of the bread and onto the table, but he kept it all under control.

"You're like a professional eater," Robin told him.

Jay laughed and still managed not to drop a crumb.

"I'm so used to eating with Wren," Robin continued, "which makes watching you even more extraordinary."

He kicked her leg playfully under the table.

It was the first time they'd been alone. Wren was up in her room, playing with her plastic horses. Mom was napping upstairs, and Dad was in the garage, contemplating his next-summer project of expanding the deck. Quentin was asleep on Robin's lap.

"You've kinda turned into a cool kid," said Jay.

"It's not like you've been gone that long. Maybe I've always been cool, but you just didn't bother to notice."

He shrugged. "Maybe."

Robin's heart swelled. They smiled at each other.

"Who knew I'd actually like having a brother again."

"Shut up." He took another bite of sandwich, and when it was thoroughly chewed and swallowed, he said, "What's up with Mom and Dad? It's weird, right?"

"Totally. I wanna blame Mom, but sometimes I wonder."

Quentin stirred in Robin's lap. He peered up at her, peeped an *I love you*, and reclosed his eyes.

"What's it like?" asked Robin. She looked up from Quentin. "To be outta here? To be free?"

He reached over and rubbed the top of Robin's head. "Awesome." He pushed into her skull until it hurt.

She shoved his hand away. "Dad's never home. It's like he's left us already."

"Shut up." As if he couldn't help himself, Jay rubbed the top of her head one more time before bringing both his hands back to his sandwich and taking a bite.

Robin wanted to say more. She wanted to beg Jay to tell her it was going to be okay, but what she was feeling was so intense that if she really tried to put it into words, it just might become real. Once something was released into the world, it was quite impossible to pretend it didn't exist. Jay was safe, already grown up enough. She had at least six more years. And Wren. What about little Wren? For the sake of the children. For heaven's sake. For God's sake. For mercy's sake. Robin decided that sake was a really weird word.

That evening, as tradition dictated, they all sat on the living room floor, the Game of Life board between them. Dad was sitting on one side of Jay, and Mom was on the other, acting like he was some sort of prize—they'd grabbed their spots before Robin had even had the chance. Dad repeatedly punched Jay in the arm, while Mom kept trying to cram more food down his throat.

"Can I get you more chips? I'm so sorry about the popcorn."

"Naw. I'm good."

Dad punched his shoulder lightly.

Robin could tell Jay wished the long weekend was over.

Wren was in her glory, totally ignoring the rules of the game and pushing around three little cars filled with pink and blue pegs. Quentin took great pleasure in stealing Wren's pegs right out of the cars and racing across the floor, peg in mouth, to drop them near Robin's knees.

"Stop it, Quentin." Wren reached over and recovered her pink peg, only to have Quentin run off with one of her blue ones. "Robin, make him stop." Wren tried to capture Quentin, but he sidestepped and fluttered onto Jay's knee.

He is so close to flying, thought Robin.

"Hey, get off of me!" Jay knocked the bird off his knee.

Quentin dropped the blue peg as he fell.

"Jay, don't push him."

"I don't want bird shit on me."

"Language, Jay."

"Bird shit. Bird shit. Bird shit," said Jay.

Wren giggled. Dad rolled his eyes, and Mom glared at Jay. Robin bet Mom was glad she had failed to buy him that popcorn.

"Whose turn is it?" asked Dad. He was restless and impatient.

Quentin shook off his tumble by ruffling his feathers and giving his body a good shake. He moved from peg stealing to one of his favorite activities—pulling shoelaces.

"I just don't see why you have to use that word," said Mom, "when poo would work just as well."

"That's total bull poo," said Jay.

Robin laughed.

"See?" Jay pointed Robin's way. "Just not the same." He gave her a conspiratorial wink.

Quentin put the end of one of Robin's shoelaces into his mouth and used his entire weight to tug, his wings spreading out with his efforts. To his delight, the bow unraveled. He moved on to her other shoe.

"Whose turn is it?" repeated Dad.

Mom sighed and reached for the spinner. "Mine."

Dad rolled his eyes. "Typical that it was you slowing things up."

Robin saw the pain flicker across Mom's face. Robin looked at Jay. He'd seen it too.

Having successfully untied both of Robin's shoes, Quentin cocked his head in search of his next bit of mischief. He jumped with excitement when he spotted the bright-green shoelaces of Jay's new running shoes.

Mom spun the spinner, momentarily causing Quentin to reconsider, but in the end, he scurried over to Jay and grabbed a mouthful of shoelace.

"Get the fuck away from my shoes." Jay kicked out his foot, sending Quentin tumbling across the game board, knocking over cars and scattering pegs all over the mountaintops.

"You're gonna hurt him."

Quentin recollected himself and ran toward Robin.

"Put him away," said Dad.

"These are brand new." Jay brushed at the laces.

Quentin jumped into Robin's lap and pushed himself deep between her crossed legs. "He's fine now," said Robin. "He'll probably go to sleep."

"Put him away," repeated Dad.

Robin appealed to Mom, who looked out a window.

"Do you have any idea what I paid for these shoes?" Jay was still messing with the laces, as if they were broken and unrepairable. "F'ing little bird."

"Fine," said Robin.

She walked slowly to the utility room. She flicked on the light, which glared off the dirty water in the sink. Mom was soaking a bathroom trash can, probably trying to get it as clean as new. Robin lifted Quentin over the top of his cardboard box, which sat on the counter near the sink, standing on her tiptoes and gently placing him near his stuffed duck. He immediately started to cry, *Don't leave me alone. Don't leave me alone.*

"I'm sorry," she told him. "They are all such jerks."

The Game of Life had nearly reached its conclusion when Quentin finally stopped chirping to get out. An hour later, Robin returned to the utility room to check on him before she went up to bed. The moment she looked over the edge of the box, her heart seemed to speed up. He wasn't tucked in next to his stuffed duck. "Quentin?"

He wasn't under his duck.

"Quentin?"

She pulled the box from the counter and onto the floor. She threw all its contents out of the box. He wasn't there. Her heart beat in her ears. She scanned the floor. Nothing. Her eyes fell on the trash can lying on its side in the utility sink filled with dirty water.

He is so close to flying.

She lifted the trash can from the water. And there he floated. Beak down. Wings out. His little body was so tiny in death—half its normal size with all his new feathers so very wet.

At some point, days later, Robin realized that not crying had nothing to do with growing up. Crying was all you could do and what you needed. Instead, growing up had everything to do with learning how to go on, day after day, with the burden of loss.

Author Note: This was one of the hardest scenes I've ever had to write. Maybe that's why I generally write fiction that's based on made-up stuff in my head and not real-life experiences. My sweet little Quentin was

my first loss, which is most likely why it hit me as hard as it did. Years later, one of my ex-boyfriends, after I told him about Quentin, insisted I hatch quail eggs again. That didn't end much better. But I was much older and better prepared.

Chapter 11: Hot Turkey!

Jay negotiated the curve like a racecar driver—too fast but with perfect control. Robin didn't fight the centripetal force. She resisted the urge to grab the handle above the side window. Her body went his way and then back against the passenger door as the car straightened. In another month, she'd get her driver's permit. Then Jay's shuttling Wren and her back and forth would eventually end. It could still be another year, though, and what if Jay finally found a job and moved out of the area? There just didn't seem to be a big demand for aeronautical engineers in Central New York.

"Do you think Mom might get her driver's license back soon?"

"She's lucky she's not in jail. I doubt it."

"A jail Byrd," said Wren from the back seat.

They all cracked up. Jay flew around another curve and dipped into another valley. Robin could feel the heat from outside through the car window. The air conditioning was working overtime, trying to compete with the hot, humid day. She checked her phone. It was ninety-eight degrees. Even though they were flying along the road, if she really looked, Robin could see tiny green apples hanging from the trees of the orchards. Another month, and they could stop at the orchards for early-fall apples.

"So, I met her the other day."

Robin turned fully around, pressed against Jay's shoulder, and looked at Wren. "You did? When?"

"When Dad picked me up from rehearsal."

Robin looked at Jay as she turned forward. She saw his eyes catch Wren's in the rearview mirror. The car slowed, and Robin wondered if he was going to pull over.

"That's fucked up," he said.

"Yeah," said Wren. "He was waiting right as I stepped out of the school like a stalker or something. When we walked to the car, he told me I'd better be nice to her."

"Are you kidding?"

"Were you?"

"Kinda. She has super-big teeth."

Robin laughed a bit too loudly. She settled back into the passenger seat.

Nobody said anything else, and Robin pressed her forehead against the window and watched the apple trees flick in and out of order—neat rows turning to scrambled clumps of green.

"She's not as pretty as Mom."

"I think Mom is super pretty," said Robin. "Especially with her new 'do. Don't you think so, Jay?"

"I can't think in those terms with my own mom."

"Mom is super pretty!" Wren's voice was high and screechy from the back seat. "Just say it!"

"Chill, Wren. Seriously." Jay sped up again like he might hurl them into the next valley.

Robin knew Jay was still really mad. Especially with Mom. Like their parents' drama had purposefully messed up his life. Dad was the one with the girlfriend now, but Mom was the one who was cheating on Dad—even if it was only with alcohol. And Jay couldn't seem to forgive her for that.

Jay was forced to slow down as he made the turn from Route 20 onto Slate Hill Road.

Robin loved Dad's new house. It was an old camp right on Otisco Lake. It was like being in a hunting cabin, fishy smelling and musky, with dark wooden walls and a large stone fireplace in the center of the main room. Even the beams holding up the roof were exposed. She and Wren got to sleep in a loft with windows that looked out over the lake. She loved the way the ladder squeaked and wobbled each time they climbed up. Watching the sun set from her tiny camp cot was her new favorite thing.

They drove through a green tunnel of corn, the stalks bending toward the road and the silky tassels waving as they passed. Red-winged black birds took flight, showing off their bright patches of color. The sky was hazy blue, not a cloud in sight. A bobolink—one of Robin's favorite birds—flew across the road. She wished Jay would slow down so she might catch the sound of their beautiful songs. Her eye spotted something at the edge of the road.

"Stop the car! Stop the car!"

"What? Why?"

"Seriously, Jay! Pull over." He began to slow, and Robin turned fully around in her seat and scanned the distant road. "There's something back there. I think it was a turkey."

The seatbelt indicator started to beep.

"A what? A turkey? F that."

"A turkey?" asked Wren. She turned to look too. "I don't see it."

Jay began to accelerate.

"No! Seriously. I think it was hurt."

"Oh my god."

"We can't just leave him."

"Fine." Jay brought the car to an abrupt stop, causing both of them to fall forward and then back. Wren nearly ended up on the floor of the car.

"Back up! Back up!"

Jay jerked the car into reverse. "Unbelievable," he said.

They went in reverse for much longer than Robin imagined was necessary. She wondered if she'd really seen anything.

"There he is!" yelled Wren.

Jay stopped the car, and Robin jumped out, followed by Wren. In the ditch at the side of the road lay a full-grown male turkey. His beak was open, his neck stretched out so that his head was nearly in the road. His beady eyes stared up at Robin. His tongue moved as he panted.

"Poor thing."

"He must have been hit by a car."

"I don't see any blood."

"Here, help me."

"Hurry up," yelled Jay from the car. "I have a date tonight."

"A date?" Robin muttered. "It's only what? Two o'clock?"

She put her hands on each side of the bird's folded wings. He didn't try to get away. Wren did likewise, but farther back, near his tail feathers. Their first attempt was a failure—neither one of them was prepared for the weight of the bird. "I suppose it would be too much to ask Jay to help us."

"We can do it," said Wren. "On three. One. Two. Three."

This time, the bird responded, his legs moving slightly, helping lift its body upward. He hung momentarily between them before they made the unspoken decision to let Robin take him.

He was heavy and damp. Robin hoped it wasn't blood. She could feel his heart beating against her chest as she walked back toward the car. He smelled slightly like a chicken coop. Wren ran up ahead and opened the passenger door.

"What the hell?" said Jay. "You're not putting that thing in the car."

Robin ignored him. She managed to sit down in the seat without dropping a feather. Wren shut the door and hopped into the back seat. With difficulty, Robin rearranged the turkey so that it was squarely in her lap. Its head was facing Jay, resting on the center console near the gear shift. He was the biggest bird Robin had ever seen.

"I can't believe my luck," she said.

Wren leaned forward between the seats and agreed. "Look how cool he is. Cooler than the pictures we looked at."

"It's gross," said Jay.

In the last couple of months, wild turkeys were some of the birds she and Wren had done a lot of reading about. Robin was especially fascinated by their heads. This guy's wattle was large and quivered as Jay put the car into drive. Its redness contrasted against the bumpy light-blue skin of its head and neck. The bird's snood popped out over his beak and was covered with pointy black hairs.

"You know, Jay, his snood can change in length and coloration depending on the circumstances."

"His what?"

"Look at it now. It's sucked up tight like a constricted blue worm." Robin pointed, almost stroking the tiny black hairs on the snood. "That's because he's hurt and scared."

"That disgusting thing coming out of his nose?"

"Above his *beak*. And it gets long and red during mating season."

"Like a penis!" yelled Wren.

Robin and Wren laughed so hard the turkey almost managed to lift his head.

"Both of you stop it. Seriously. That blue head is absurd. And that snoot or whatever you said..." Jay shook his head and shoulders as if a chill had just gone through him. "What are we doing with that thing? Thanksgiving is still months away."

"Funny." Robin tapped the bird's head. His blue eyelids slid closed and then reopened. "The vet down the road also does bird rehab. Remember we took those baby wood ducks to him? We'll take Mr. Tom there."

"Yeah!" said Wren.

"You're both ridiculous," said Jay. He began to drive, slowly now, as if he were trying to make up his mind. The air conditioning blew through the car, quickly cooling the hot air that had forced its way in when they'd stopped for the bird.

"Dad will totally freak if he gets a vet bill," said Jay.

"Poor Mr. Tom," said Wren. "We have to help him."

"It's wild-bird rehab," said Robin. "There won't be a charge." Robin stroked the silky black iridescent feathers along Mr. Tom's back.

They drove on for another mile, saying nothing.

The turkey's beating heart seemed to slow. He closed his beak, put his head up, and looked around. He shifted in Robin's lap. She felt the claws of his feet contract and then spread out. His talons latched onto her thighs.

"Ow!" She tried to hold him tighter. His snood began to pulsate and grow red and angry looking. "Uh-oh."

"What?" said Wren. "Is he worse? Is he going to die?" Her voice cracked like she was about to cry.

Mr. Tom raised his head higher and turned toward Robin. Their eyes met. His face was inches away from hers. His wings pushed against her hands. The talons squeezed deeper into her thighs.

"Stop the car! Stop the car!"

This time, Jay listened to her immediately. Before the car came to a full stop, Robin pushed open the door and shoved Mr. Tom right on out. His wings spread, and he disappeared into the corn.

"Oh my god!" She looked at the red marks on her thighs. The skin was just broken. Small beads of blood formed like red candy dots. "I guess he was just hot."

Jay looked at her legs and began to laugh.

"He was seriously about to kill me!"

Wren began to laugh. Robin wiped away the blood and joined in. They all got to laughing so hard that Jay had to pull the car over again. Soon, tears were streaming down their faces.

Once she was able to talk, Robin said, "You know what? I think I'm really going to enjoy this year's Thanksgiving turkey. Even if we *are* forced to eat two of them at two different places."

Author Note: This chapter was based on my experience with picking up a full-grown male turkey off the side of the road. Believe me, when he started to recover from what must have been heatstroke, I couldn't get him out of the car fast enough. In my experience, the two most terrifying birds are roosters and male wild turkeys. I hear ganders can be pretty scary, too, but luckily, I don't have firsthand knowledge of them.

Chapter 12: A Walk in the Woods

Robin loved to walk in the woods across from Dad's new house on the lake. The trees were old, with huge trunks and branches too high to climb. The canopy was thick enough to cool the midsummer day, which had continued to be hotter than normal. Where there had been so many spring flowers just a few short weeks ago was now mainly a layer of leaves from the fall. The trout-lilies and trillium had disappeared. The forest floor no longer crunched with each step. It was no longer slimy-slippery from spring. It was firm and gave off a wonderful woodsy smell as she walked. The fruit of the mayapple was dark yellow. The jack-in-the-pulpit berries were turning bright red. Summer was at its full glory. Robin didn't want it to ever end.

A huge bird took flight above her head, which caused her to look up and accidentally kick a puff mushroom. Black spores exploded around her. She laughed, almost overcome with joy.

She'd seen a boy at the park and then again just a few minutes ago at the little convenience store down the street. He'd smiled at her, his blue eyes flashing mischief, his teeth whiter than the whitest cloud. Rumor was his name was Aiden, and he was renting a camp on the lake with his family for the summer. A miraculous beautiful boy.

She glanced behind her, as she had done many times since slipping into these woods. She imagined him stepping out into the open from behind a tree trunk. Yes, he had followed her here. His smile would be the brightest thing in the forest. He'd come toward her, her body feeling each of his steps across the leaves. He would take her hand and lean in for a kiss so sweet, so gentle. Everything a first kiss should be. She thought of bluebirds and butterflies, of the soft waves of her hair blowing in the summer breeze, and of the tiny hint of moisture that would be on his lips as they parted.

Robin dropped to the ground, her knees against the old leaves, dapples of sunlight fluttering along the forest, and she began to laugh. She was being absurd. Another fantasy ran through her head that he was behind her now, watching her laugh. This made her laugh all the more. Her life had been so much less bizarre when all she'd cared about were birds. But now that bees had been thrown into the mix, she barely knew what to do with herself. The thought of the birds and bees sent a wave of what could only be desire through her. She resisted the urge to clutch at her newly formed breasts and push against the closest stump, reminding herself that it was only crazy teenage hormones.

She spent a few more minutes on the floor of the forest, shifting through the leaves and uncovering roly-poly bugs, tiny worms, little spiders, and even a small red-backed salamander, before getting up and heading for the creek. These creatures—all these amazing little creatures and their worlds that surrounded her—seemed to help still her other needs. Crayfish would surely squelch them.

Robin made her way up the creek bed, wading in the current, which was flowing harder than normal from yesterday's thunderstorms. This proved a problem for her crayfish hunt. Either the water was too fast and bubbly to see clearly when she lifted a rock, or when she did think she saw a beautiful brown crustacean, it was quickly swept away before she had any chance of snagging it. She moved farther up the creek to where it widened and straightened until she found a side pool of calmer water. She lifted one rock and then another. Under rock number three, she uncovered the grandpapa of crayfish. He'd curled his tail up under him, ready to slingshot away. He'd raised his pincers, ready for battle. She knew he hadn't grown this big and lived this long because he was a fool.

She waited for the water to clear completely. They watched each other. What did she look like in his eyes? Was she a clear image? Did she look like a monster? Like God? She did not wish to be either. Her eyes narrowed, and she puckered her lips in determination. Her aim was true, and she nabbed him right behind the eyes. She lifted him to eye level, drops of water falling from his body. His pincers swung every which way, but try as he might, her fingers were just out of reach.

"Hi, there, Mr. Crayfish. Did I shake up your day?"

The faint snap of his pincers banging shut, just audible over the moving water, was suddenly overridden by another sound. She looked away from her prey and in the direction of the noise, causing a momentary shift of her fingers. "Ow!" She dropped Mr. Crayfish, noted her bloody wound, put her finger to her mouth, and stepped closer to the sound. "What the heck is that?" she asked the trees.

Upstream, approaching quickly, was the smallest bit of brown fuzz, and it was peeping hysterically.

"A duck?" she asked. "A tiny baby duck?"

And sure enough, the little creature frantically paddled right up to her. Robin bent over quickly and scooped her up before she was swept right on by.

The bird was hardly bigger than a golf ball. Her belly was nearly white. Her body was covered with tiny black-and-white feathers. Her chin was creamy white, and her head was topped with a black tuft of feathers, like a cute miniature mohawk.

"You're a baby merganser," whispered Robin. "Where's your mama?"

Robin tucked the little duck in to her chest and walked up and down the stream, listening carefully for the sound of other baby ducks or a call from Mama. After ten minutes, she gave up.

"Guess I have no choice other than to bring you home."

The baby duck's frantic calls had softened to a gentle peep. She looked up at Robin and cocked her head to one side as if to get a better view of her new mom. The bond was instant and mutual.

"And I shall call you Maxine because you are clearly the greatest little duck ever."

Aiden, if that was truly the boy's name, didn't enter Robin's thoughts again—at least for the rest of that particular day.

Author Note: Years ago, when my youngest daughter, Sarah, was home from college, she found Maxine in the woods across from our house on Otisco Lake. The hooded merganser and bufflehead are two of the most striking of the wild ducks that spent time on our little lake. Like the wood duck, mergansers nest in cavities of large trees. Within twenty-four hours of hatching, their mama calls for them to drop to the ground, sometimes as far as fifty feet, and follow her to the nearest body of water.

Chapter 13: Duck, Duck, Boy

Robin opened the door of the cooler and welcomed the blast of cold air. If the convenience store had an air conditioner, it wasn't working properly. She knew she wanted a Go Banana Snapple, but she lingered as if she were unsure just to receive a few more seconds of cool. K&L Convenience wasn't like a regular minimart. A converted old farmhouse, K&L had everything from drainpipes to lollipops. One could find peanut butter, fishing line, ice cream, steel screws, mouse traps, fresh wiggly bait, dust-covered cans of tomato soup, cases of beer stacked to the ceiling, PVC piping of every dimension, and slices of pretty decent freshly made pizza with lots of stringy cheese.

All the locals seemed to know each other, and Robin loved to hang and listen to the gossip. She walked carefully to the front of the store, trying not to disturb Maxine, who had finally fallen to sleep against her chest under her T-shirt. She was tucked in above Robin's breasts, her bra helping keep the little duck in place. She twisted open her drink, took a sip, and began to peruse the cork bulletin board near the doorway. There was always someone offering some sort of service or awards for the return of an unlucky lost dog or cat. Once there had even been a lost cow. A three-hundred-dollar reward. Robin would have loved to know the story behind that.

The door jingled as someone entered the store. "Hi, Al," said Kevin.

Kevin was the owner along with his wife, Laura. Thus, the K&L. Robin was embarrassed that it had taken her months to figure that one out. Kevin spent most of his time running around various places in the store and on the property, but this afternoon he was manning the counter.

"Morning." Al was a large man dressed in dirty blue jeans and a dirty white T-shirt that was ripped and full of holes from years of use. He wore a John Deere cap, and Robin guessed by the smell of him that he owned one of the local dairy farms.

"How's Jenna?" asked Kevin.

Robin leaned a little toward the conversation. She didn't know Al and, to her knowledge, had never seen Jenna, but she did know Jenna had had an unfortunate encounter with a rooster yesterday.

"Eight stitches," answered Al. He smiled. "And one pretty darn good chicken stew."

The men's laughter woke Maxine with a start. She nearly fell off the shelf of Robin's bra and right out the bottom of her shirt.

Robin tucked her shirt into her shorts, readjusted Maxine, and rubbed the duck's downy head. "It's okay," Robin whispered. She was trying to prevent a full-on duck anxiety attack. She really didn't want Maxine to start in with the panic peeping, as Robin called it.

Maxine, like no other baby bird—not even Quentin—was a twenty-four, seven job. Robin couldn't even go to the bathroom alone. If Maxine wasn't being held or right under her feet, the bird would panic peep, flap her stubby little wings, and run after Robin just as fast as her big black feet would go. Sometimes she would get going so fast, she'd trip over her own feet. It was exhausting being a duck mom.

Wren wasn't around this week to help and had shown zero interest in the pictures Robin had texted her. Maybe it was a good thing, because lately they seemed to be fighting more than getting along. Sharing bird-parenting duties, as they always had in the past, might add to the stress.

Robin believed she was smoothly transitioning into adulthood; she was more or less accepting of her annoying adolescence, while Wren seemed to be fighting it with all she had. Always wanting to be at Mom's, Wren had flatly refused to spend the scheduled week at Dad's.

Aren't you excited to meet Maxine? Robin had texted her this morning.

Wren had yet to send a response.

It was unbelievable that Wren didn't want to meet the cutest baby duck ever. Robin was tempted to refuse to go back to Mom's Sunday night. Maxine needed her daily swimming lessons. Dad seemed to really love Maxine. Even Jay had been texting her daily for duck updates. Robin knew that Dad was hurt by the way Wren was acting. Even though it was nice having Dad all to herself, it made her mad that Wren had hurt him.

As tiring and as demanding as Maxine could be, Robin had never felt more loved or needed. Maybe what Wren needed was a duck of her own. She mused about the possibility of staying with Dad another week, peering at Maxine as she continued to stroke the lovely head. Maxine's eyes began to flutter closed.

The door jingled again. Robin looked up. The boy whose name might be Aiden walked in, catching Robin with her hand down her shirt.

"Hey," he said.

Robin nearly dropped her Snapple.

Maxine let out a series of tiny peeps in response.

The boy's eyebrows went up and then almost touched each other. "Got something interesting in there?" he asked.

Robin wasn't sure if she was amused or annoyed. The way he said the words and the look on his face creeped her out, but at the same time, a pleasant little twinge pulsed through her. She stood a little taller and said, "Maxine. She's a baby hooded merganser. She's approximately four days old." As if on cue, Maxine popped her head out from the top of Robin's T-shirt and cocked her head at the boy.

"Say whaaat?"

All Robin's confusion evaporated. She laughed with delight. She loved the way he'd said those words. His hair was dark—almost black—and in need of a trim, curling at the tips, which nearly reached his shoulders. His eyes were really more hazel than brown. What was especially cute was the splattering of tiny freckles all over his face—like his hair really should have been red. "Is your name Aiden?"

"Andy."

"Andy?"

"Yeah." He looked a little embarrassed that his name wasn't Aiden. "But enough about me..." He paused, waiting for her to give him her name.

"Robin."

"Robin." His eyes flicked up as if he were filing away her name, before coming right back as if he would never look away again. "Like the bird?"

She met his gaze. "Robin Aletta Byrd." She'd long gotten over her dislike of her name, and now her attitude hovered around arrogant pride.

It was his turn to laugh. "Well, I was gonna say that I'd never met a girl with a duck down her shirt, but now I see it all kinda makes sense."

"Exactly."

And it was right there and then that Robin fell in love for the second time in a week. First with the best little duck ever and now with a boy whose name wasn't Aiden.

Author Note: Hooded mergansers are one of the most beautiful and talented diving ducks. They pursue their prey, such as fish and crayfish, with great gusto and can stay under water for close to two minutes. They are equally skilled in flight, reaching up to fifty miles per hour, but not so impressive on land. Because their legs are positioned farther back on

their bodies and their feet are extra-large, they walk like a drunk scuba diver trying to make his way up the beach.

Chapter 14: Quagmire

Andy and Robin sat at the edge of the lake, their toes exploring the combination of rocks, mud, and leaf debris. Every once in a while, their toes would find each other in the quag, sending ripples of pleasure through Robin's body.

The baby duck was beyond delighted with the outing. Honing her diving skills, Maxine peeped with enthusiasm, flapped her tiny wings, tucked them tightly, and submerged her entire body, using her beak to push through the mud and snap up any possible edible plants, bugs, or tiny crustaceans their toes unearthed. Robin and Andy watched in silence as she dived over and over. Her little tail sometimes popped up in the air, but mostly she was learning to stay longer and longer underwater, kicking her big feet with all she had.

"Do you think she even peeps underwater?" asked Andy.

"Probably." Robin's right big toe touched the top of Andy's foot. Neither of them moved. Robin looked away from Maxine and into Andy's eyes. "I really like the word quag."

He blinked at her. "As in quagmire?"

She bit her lower lip and nodded. Even with the coolness of the water and mud, she could feel the heat of Andy's foot below her toe.

"Mire is a cool word too."

"True," whispered Robin.

Then she did something funny with her face and mouth. Andy's face changed too. This was it. The moment of her first kiss. All those times practicing on her hand, that time she kissed her mom good night a little too long just to see what it would be like, all those scenes from movies and shows and videos online—all of this flashed through her head as Andy's face got closer. She pressed a little harder with her big toe, feeling the give in Andy's foot. He placed his other foot on top of hers, making a foot sandwich. His hand went to her shoulder. A tiny slit appeared between his lips, and she lost focus on his eyes. His mouth was warm and slightly wet. She wasn't totally sure what to do with hers. She moved her lips ever so slightly, and to her astonishment, he thrust his tongue into her mouth and swept it around like you might the inside of an ice cream cone.

It was gross.

He tightened his hold on her shoulder and brought his other hand to her stomach, under her T-shirt, and started inching up toward her breasts. His tongue tasted like an old taco. She wanted to bite it—hard. Her own tongue contracted. It was trying to find a place to hide. She brought her hands to his chest to push him away just as his hand shoved its way under her bra and grabbed her left breast.

Maxine squeaked with excitement and leaped from the water and onto Robin's thigh. Robin could feel her big wet feet. Then she must have given herself a good shake, because they were both sprayed with droplets of muddy water. Andy released his hold just enough to allow Robin to gracefully break away. Robin looked at his face. Half of it was covered with watery mud, and she laughed. Whether from anxiety or real mirth, she laughed so hard that she snorted a couple of times.

This seemed to thrill Maxine, who ran up her thigh and onto her stomach then tried repeatedly to scramble up her chest, aiming, no doubt, to slip down her shirt.

Andy brushed his face. Robin didn't care that half her face was also wet. She scooped up Maxine and let her crawl down her shirt. A wet duck was sure to keep Andy away. Maxine peeped with happiness. Her little wings and feet pushed out Robin's shirt in every direction as she tried to bury herself in Robin's bra. Her peeping was constant and content.

It was only then that Robin wiped her face—first at her lips to wipe away what Andy had left behind and then at the mud she could feel on her cheek and chin. So, this was it—what would always be her first kiss. Andy must have seen it on her face, because he looked away in what looked like shame.

"I didn't mean—" He mumbled the words, shifting his foot deep within the quagmire. "I mean, I'm sorry."

He looked so lost, so embarrassed, and so sincere that a wave of guilt washed over Robin. Was it really his fault? Could he even help his desire to cram his tongue down her throat and paw at her breast? Wasn't it really her own fault? After all, they were just popping right out there.

Maxine snugged her wet body farther down and gently nibbled almost seductively on Robin's right nipple. Before she quite knew what was happening, Robin brought her hands to each side of Andy's face and gave him the kind of kiss she had wanted—gentle and slow—the way Maxine was nibbling on her nipple. He responded in kind, and every part of Robin melted into him. She broke away, just at the right time, before the need for him to paw at her breast again overcame all reason.

She stood up, cradling Maxine through her shirt with one hand, and put the other on her hip. "And that, Andy Jacob, is how it's done." Then she walked away, leaving him with his mouth slightly open and his feet in the quagmire.

*A*uthor Note: I wonder how many people actually receive a first kiss that matches or exceeds their imagination. Mine certainly didn't. One of my very early childhood fears was that I might die from some tragic childhood illness before I found someone willing to kiss me. This seems silly now but also pretty darn sad.*

Chapter 15: Ducks, Dads, and Boys

"How's Maxine today?" Dad asked as he put the pizza box on the table. "Sorry, we're having pizza again. I know I said I'd be home early enough to cook something spectacular with you." He tugged on his tie to loosen it. He must have had an important meeting today because he didn't usually wear a tie to work.

Robin shrugged. "I made a salad. I even put baby spinach in it." Maxine nuzzled deeper in between Robin's thighs. "She's really getting good at swimming. You should see how she dives."

"You can show me tomorrow. Maybe we can all swim together."

Tomorrow was Saturday, so Dad didn't have to go to work, which made Robin unhappy on several fronts. First, it meant that the next day—Sunday—she'd have to go back to Mom's. How would Maxine continue her swimming lessons in Mom's tiny apartment in Syracuse? Robin certainly wasn't looking forward to sharing the super-small bedroom with Wren. Someday she and Wren would hopefully grow close again, but for now, Robin had way too much going on to try to deal with it. Then there was Andy. His family was leaving early next week, going back to Brooklyn. How could she spend time with him with Dad hanging around all day tomorrow? The only answer was to stay at Dad's an extra week, solving every dilemma. Maxine could swim, and Wren and her bad attitude could go screw themselves. And best of all, she and Andy would have all day Monday and part of Tuesday alone.

Dad pulled his tie off fully and threw it toward the kitchen counter. It balanced momentarily at the edge and then sailed to the floor. He shrugged, sat down at the table, and opened the pizza box. He chose the piece with the most pepperoni. "Here ya go, Robby," he said, putting it on her plate. Robin usually loved it when Dad called her Robby, but something about the way he said it kicked her into high alert.

"Salad?" she asked, passing him the bowl.

"Absolutely!"

Uh-oh.

She hesitated at the handoff. They both looked at each other.

"What's up?" she asked.

Dad took the salad bowl from her and set it down next to his plate. He rubbed his upper lip gently, as if he were contemplating a proposal for world peace. "I know—or it's my impression that your mom—" He hesitated again, and Robin really started to panic. "That maybe she hasn't necessarily been proactive in... telling you what you might need to know about..."

"Aardvarks?" Robin offered.

Dad laughed. "Now, Robin, I'm trying to have a serious conversation here."

Robin nodded solemnly. "Aardvarks are seriously serious."

Dad sighed. "Okay, here's the thing. I ran into Charlie out in the driveway." Charlie shared the same lake lane with Dad's house. He was a total crank and seemed to have an aversion to wearing shirts. Not seeing his huge pot belly was the only thing making Robin long for summer to end and the cooler temps of winter. "He said he saw you down by the lake..."

Robin couldn't help it. She felt her eyes widen.

"Sucking on some boy's face."

"Sucking on some boy's face? *On* his face? Oh my god!"

Dad sat back and crossed his arms over his chest. "That was the gist of it, yes."

Robin was mortified. "Unbelievable!" She stood up fast, knocking Maxine to the floor. As she swooped down to pick up the little duck, having every intention of stomping out of the room, Dad placed his hand firmly on her shoulder, forcing her back into her seat.

"Not so fast."

Robin huffed her annoyance. This had all the makings of being worse than the time he'd given her a lecture about the proper disposal of tampons.

"Now, face sucking," said Dad, "while natural and fun, has its drawbacks."

"Kill me. Just kill me now."

He put up a finger. "One, germs." Up came his second finger. "Two, skin burn from stubble. Three, chapped lips."

Robin put her head down on the table and banged it lightly repeatedly.

"Four."

"Dad, stop," she mumbled into the table.

"Four. Most importantly, four. Face sucking leads to—and I think you know the word. Sex. S. E. X."

He was on a roll now, in full lecture mode. If Robin didn't do something fast, he'd be grabbing one of the bananas from the kitchen counter and showing her how to put a condom on it.

"Now, as I said when we started, I'm not sure if your mom has properly prepared you—"

She lifted her head off the table. "Dad! I know! I know all about S. E. X. See? I can even spell it. Penis. Vagina. I know it all."

He waved his hand her way, commanding her attention. "Words are great, Robin. Birth control is great. Protection from STDs is great. But what you don't know, may never fully understand, is how little boys—and even a lot of men—really care about you. About *you*. Y. O. U. At the end of the day, the cliché that boys only want one thing is absolute fact."

Robin thought about the fact that Dad had left Mom for another woman and was already on his third girlfriend since the split. She thought about all the many, many girls Jay had been with and the mean things he often had to say about them, during and after the fact. She thought about the way Andy's eyes and hands had gone right to her breasts. She thought about how few questions he'd actually asked her over the last few days and how his eyes seemed to glaze over when she got to talking about birds or her career plans or her family history. But what she thought and said were two different things.

"Well maybe, just maybe," she said, tucking Maxine into her chest with one hand and pushing up from the table with the other, "I only want *one* thing too!" And with that, she was gone, out of the room and up the loft ladder. It was a shame that Dad didn't have a proper stairway to stomp up or a proper door to slam.

Author Note: Birds and bees are extremely complicated, mingled with so many nuances, complications, consequences, and expectations. And that's how it is for adults. For young people just navigating love, sex, and heartache... well, it would be so much easier if we were all ducks.

Chapter 16: Duck Versus Boy

Quintessential was Robin's new favorite word, and today was a quintessential summer day. She'd made a point of using quintessential three times in the last few hours. Once with Andy in a text, once with Dad, and another time during a phone call with Mom. The lake sparkled under a sky of the bluest blue. The humidity was low. The temperature was just hot enough to make the waters of the lake refreshing without making you want to jump right back in as soon as you came out.

A perfect quintessential Saturday afternoon, except for one thing. So far, Robin had failed to convince Mom or Dad to let her stay at the lake another week. Maxine's swimming lessons just didn't seem to be a convincing-enough argument with either of them. Robin strongly suspected that they were in cahoots to keep her away from Andy, which was so unfair. Her parents had finally agreed—and were working together on something—but it had to be at her expense. What if Andy was the one? A missed opportunity that she'd regret the rest of her life. If nothing else, she at least wanted to feel those lips again.

The three of them had been swimming for the last hour—Dad, Maxine, and Robin. They had splashed, laughed, and pretended to have fun, but it was hard for Robin to embrace this rare time with Dad or the delight of every milestone that Maxine was making in her short six days of life.

"Look at that little duck go," said Dad.

He was reclining on one of those silly-looking floating water chairs with the cup holders at the ends of both arm rests. It gave the ability to be double "fisted" with your beer while you swam. His cup holders were empty. She hadn't seen Dad drink since the split with Mom.

He wiggled his feet toward Maxine. "She's a regular diving pro. I'd stick close to her, though. Don't let her get too far from where you are. I wouldn't want something to gobble her up."

"I know," Robin said, dipping her head under the water and then flipping her hair out of her face.

It seemed impossible to let Maxine get too far away. The little duck stuck to her like glue. Robin eased onto the raft, and Maxine scurried up after, pushing against Robin's thigh.

Robin picked her up and kissed her wet head. "I love this little duck," she said.

"I agree. She's pretty darn special."

Maxine peeped and peeped. She nibbled at the skin under Robin's chin until it nearly hurt.

"She's turning into a real duck," he continued. "You're doing a great job with her."

"Thanks," said Robin. "So maybe you're starting to see how staying here by the lake is better for Maxine?"

"Oh please. Do not bring that up again. A bathtub or Mom's big metal container will work just fine. And be safer. Maxine still has a lot of growing to do before she really needs lake-swimming skills."

Robin sighed. "It's just not fair."

"You're more than welcome to ask this boy over this afternoon."

And there it was—proof that this was Andy and nothing else. How lame would it be to have Andy over with Dad chaperoning like this was the eighteenth century or something?

"I don't even want to see him," Robin said a bit louder than she'd intended.

"Right."

"Right!"

Dad kicked his feet and moved his arms until he'd turned the chair around and headed for the dock. "I have a quick phone call I need to make. Can I bring you something from the house when I return?"

"Nope."

He flipped his foot and sent a spray of water into her face. "Nope?"

Robin sighed. "No, thank you. I meant no, thank you."

As soon as Dad disappeared up the steps leading to the house, Robin paddled back to the shore. She shook off her hands enough to grab her phone without getting it wet and checked her home screen for any texts. There were notifications for three texts, all from Andy. Water dripped from her hair and onto the screen, making it impossible to unlock her phone. She plopped Maxine down near the edge of the lake and ran for her towel. Maxine's peeping intensified as she waddled after Robin. *Don't leave me! Don't leave me!* she peeped.

"Dude, I'm just getting my towel," she told the duck.

Robin went up one step to retrieve the towel that was hanging on the stair rail. Maxine leapt repeatedly against the step, her little wings useless.

"Sometimes… Sometimes you're a bit too much," Robin said as she returned to the edge of the lake, towel in hand. She used one end to give Maxine a quick rubdown and the other to dry herself before sitting them both down on the towel and giving her phone another go. Maxine calmed down immediately, peeping softly and nuzzling Robin's legs.

Sup

Just chillin' here

I'm a little lonely

Those were the three texts Andy had sent while Robin was swimming with Dad.

I'm a little lonely

Robin read it over and over again. She started to text back a happy emoji but decided that was stupid. She made several false attempts at an appropriate response and finally settled on: *Sup back at ya*

She regretted it immediately. What did that even mean?

Andy responded within seconds. *Meet me at the park.*

My dad is stalking me.

Bring him too. Then a winky face.

Robin smiled and typed her response. Maxine pushed against her leg and tried to get in her lap. *You have a thing for dads?*

Ha ha

Maxine's peeping went up a notch.

My dad's pretty cute.

As cute as you?

Maxine chirped excitedly as a small dragonfly hovered near the shore. She went to investigate, wading into the water and stretching out her neck in its direction. When it flew away, she contented herself with pushing through shallow waters, shoving her head between the rocks. The waves of a boat rocked in. Maxine bobbed up and down in the moving water, her constant peeping heard over the sounds of the swells.

"He thinks I'm cute," whispered Robin.

Before she had a chance to come up with a snappy reply, dots appeared on her screen as Andy was writing. He wrote for a long time.

I really like you. It's quintessential that I see you today.

Robin didn't care that he'd used quintessential inappropriately. Everything was still and quiet. Even Robin's heart seemed to stop for just a moment as she read his words.

But when it decided to beat again, it was with a hard bang. Because it was quiet. For the first time in six days, there was not a peep to be heard. Robin looked up from her phone. "Maxine?" The lake was nearly flat. "Maxine?" She dropped her phone and stood up. "Maxine!" Robin scanned the shore. She scanned as far as her eyes could see. She fully searched the land near the lake then waded into the water and looked beneath.

"Dad!" Robin pushed away rocks, searching through the quagmire. Tears were running down Robin's face. "Dad!"

Maxine was nowhere.

"Dad!"

Author Note: In Eckhart Tolle's book The Power of Now, *he talks about how the ancient seers of India saw the world as a divine game that God is playing. He goes on to say that in this game, the individual life forms are not all that critical. The world is a "molecular dance." He's further quoted as saying "Life is the dancer, and you are the dance."*

Chapter 17: The Power of Loss

In the end, Robin got what she'd wanted. She stayed at Dad's another week. She spent that time mostly crying in bed. When she wasn't in bed, she was down at the lake, calling Maxine. When she wasn't crying or searching the lake, she was dreaming about Maxine. Her dreams were primarily auditory. The first time she'd heard Maxine in her dreams, she jumped out of bed, made her way down the loft stairs, ran out onto the deck overlooking the lake, and listened carefully. There was nothing but the night noises. She fell to the deck flooring and sobbed until Dad woke and gathered her up. She'd spent the remainder of the night sleeping in Dad's bed like a tiny broken child.

Three weeks later, Dad took Robin, Wren, and Jay out for a fancy dinner at the Krebs in Skaneateles to celebrate Jay's new job at Lockheed Martin. It might not have been his dream job in aeronautical engineering, like NASA or SpaceX, but Robin could tell both Dad and Jay were thrilled. Dad had strayed from his new protocol regarding drinking and ordered a bottle of champagne. He'd even gone so far as to persuade their waiter to bring four delicate crystal flutes and poured just a tiny splash of bubbly in Wren's and hers.

Robin lifted her glass, smiling at her family. The room was lovely. The old house had been turned into a restaurant long ago but had stayed true to its origins. The room they were seated in, which had once been the living room, was elegant and charming, tastefully decorated without being over-the-top or snooty, and filled with enticing aromas. Robin, for the first time in weeks, was feeling all right—almost happy.

"To Jay," said Dad. "You've always been a bit of a putz, but let it be known for all to hear that I have never doubted that someday, somehow, some way, you'd achieve greatness!" He winked at Robin. "It's just unclear when the hell that'll be!"

Everyone laughed.

But then Dad grew serious. "Truly, Jay, congrats. You're going to knock 'em dead at Lockheed."

They clicked their glasses.

The champagne made Robin's nose tickle as she brought it to her lips. She'd had champagne the New Year's before. Mom had let her have an entire glass. It had been amazing how fast she felt dizzy, like the bubbles had gone right to her brain. She tossed down what was in her glass then put out her glass for more. Dad just laughed and refilled his and Jay's.

"It's not fair." Wren was sitting on Robin's right. She leaned in and gave Robin a little nudge with her shoulder. "Mom would give us the entire bottle," she whispered in Robin's ear.

"Exactly," said Robin. But truth be told, she felt... *What is it? Safer?* She felt safer with Dad. Not that there was anything specific that was making her feel unsafe. At least, she didn't think there was. She tilted up her glass one more time and managed to knock loose another drop or two.

Wren did the same before she set her glass back down and turned toward Robin. "I'm sorry about Maxine." It was the first time she'd mentioned the loss of the little duck.

Robin blinked at her in true surprise. "Thank you. So am I."

Wren had recently changed her look again. Just last week, she'd had her hair cut super short and dyed it the blackest black. Her makeup was a cross between goth and emo. Her clothing reminded Robin of a clown's. Sitting next to her sister, Robin was sure she looked like unsalted mashed potatoes on a stick with her off-white top and black leggings. Maybe it was time for Robin to become a little more adventurous in her clothing choices. "I'm liking your ensemble," Robin said, waving her hands over Wren's body. "Maybe I need a little change too."

Wren smiled with true pleasure. "I can let you borrow anything you'd like." Robin couldn't remember why she'd had such an issue with Wren recently.

Loss was an odd thing. Maxine's loss especially was mixed with so much guilt, grief, and disbelief. Even more than the loss of Quentin. Robin couldn't imagine surviving what some might call a true loss, like losing one of her family members. She had spent the last couple of weeks thinking about that a lot.

Loss is something that can't be measured by the perceived value of what is lost, she'd written in her notebook. She'd underlined it three times.

The little duck had touched her life for a mere six days, but in her heart, she knew that the grief she felt after losing Maxine could get no deeper—even if the loss had been a family member. But she believed she was getting through it faster than if had been a human loss. It felt good to be getting on the other side of the guilt, grief, and disbelief. She had almost stopped listening for peeps while near the shore.

"What's everyone getting?" asked Dad, interrupting Robin's musings.

Everybody grew quiet as they scanned the menu.

Robin wasn't sure what she was in the mood for. "Maybe the scallops," she said.

Jay set his menu down with authority and took another sip of champagne. "I'm getting the duck."

Robin's heart jumped. She took in a quick influx of air. Dad's eyes met hers across the table.

"What?" asked Jay.

"Duck, Jay? Really?" asked Wren.

"Oh. Right. Too soon?"

"Too soon," said Dad.

Robin drew a long, deep breath and managed a smile. "It's okay." She picked up her empty glass and brought it closer to Dad. "Please, just a little more. For another toast."

Dad nodded ever so slightly and poured small amounts into everyone's glasses.

"To Maxine," said Robin. "To her short and beautiful life."

"To Maxine," her family said.

Tiny tings filled the air as they brought their glasses together.

In the end, Jay ordered a filet mignon.

And what of the boy whose name wasn't Aiden?

Much like Maxine, Robin never saw him again.

Author Note: The real Maxine was found by my daughter one summer when she was home from college, and after the little duck disappeared, both of us were crushed. While my daughter was the main caregiver for Maxine, letting her sleep in the bed with her and poop all over the sheets, I was like a daddy duck, stepping in when needed. Ten years later, we still mourn that little duck. Maxine was one bright speck of life that touched our lives and expanded forever our definition of love.

Chapter 18: One Wedding, Two Lovers, Four Ducks

Christina looked incredible in the simple off-white dress. It was tea length and perfect for an outdoor wedding. She wore an old-fashioned wide-brimmed hat the same color as the dress—the only splash of color being her bright-red hair. Even her bouquet was an array of off-white flowers with just a hint of green. It was a rare warm and sunny spring day—early April generally being a continuation of winter's cold with rain and mud thrown into the mix. But the temperature was close to seventy, and the sky was bright blue. Robin could hardly hear the processional music over the sounds of birds.

Robin squeezed Matthew's arm a little tighter and turned her gaze back toward Jay. "He looks so happy," she whispered into Matthew's ear.

"Who could blame him? Look how hot she is."

Robin shoved Matthew playfully in his arm with her shoulder. He leaned over and kissed her. They'd been together for nearly two years, having met in the middle of Robin's junior year as a premed student at SUNY Binghamton. They'd told each other they loved each other, but soon she'd be going off to Cornell to study veterinary medicine and he off to Boston for graduate work in physics. Even though they hadn't quite gotten around to putting it into exact words, they both knew their relationship was unlikely to survive. Nonetheless, she pulled him in and returned the kiss in an inappropriate way, considering where they were and who they were with.

Dad sat immediately to her left, next to his new wife, Ann. Robin liked her well enough. Her only resentment was that Dad had given up the lake cottage and moved to a big house in Manlius. Wren sat to Robin's right, next to Mom, who was sitting with her new man friend—which Robin was pretty sure was just for show. He was probably some guy she'd dragged here from her AA group. It had been years since Mom had dated anyone, working more on herself than relationships. But it seemed to be doing the trick. As far as Robin knew, Mom had been sober for four years now. A record. She had a new job in marketing she loved and had just moved into a new apartment complex where the buildings were in a circle, surrounding a pretty little pond. Maybe Robin had lost the lakefront of Dad's old house, but at least when she visited Mom, there were ducks and other watery creatures.

The wedding ceremony was short and poignant. By the end, nearly everyone was crying, as if it were a funeral rather than a celebration of marriage. Huge tears were rolling down Jay's cheeks.

Robin blotted her eyes and whispered in Matthew's ear, "He's probably crying like that because he's just committed to not sleeping with other women for the rest of his life."

Matthew laughed but not to the extent that Robin wanted. Was their relationship already dying? Even though it was only April?

Suddenly Wren had her by the arm and was dragging her away. "Quick! We need to point people to the bar and tell the band to get ready."

Ever since Jay had announced his engagement, Wren had been organizing the wedding. Robin didn't think Christina had had any say at all. Even Christina's mom—the mother of the bride—was told what color dress she was to wear. But Robin had to admit, so far, everything was perfect—the venue, the flower arrangements, the color scheme, the weather, everything.

"I think you've found your calling," Robin said to Wren as they made their way from the wedding site to the tent where the reception was to be held. And Wren really needed something, having refused to go to college and still working at the local Dunkin' Donuts, a job she had started in high school. At least she'd finally been promoted to assistant manager.

"Everything is amazing—so far."

"Shut up! Don't jinx me!"

Wren had picked out a soft teal dress for Robin, which was proving a bit of a challenge. It was sleeveless, without even clear straps, so Robin was forced to go braless. She was constantly pushing up the padded fabric, for fear her breasts would pop right out or the dress would fall right off. "I need some adhesive or something," said Robin as Wren forced her into a trot.

"Oh! I have double-sided tape. I'll get it for you just as soon as the band starts."

Late that night, in the guest bathroom of Mom's new apartment, Robin gently pulled the tape from the fabric, letting the dress fall to the floor and then from each of her breasts.

"You need some help with that?" Matthew came up from behind her and ran his fingers up her back, slipped them forward, and cupped a hand over each breast. He smelled of whiskey and sweat from hours of drinking and dancing, but rather than grossing her out, the odor swept over her in a wave of desire. She pressed back into him and stole a glance at the two of them in the bathroom mirror. Her breasts weren't quite visible under his hands, her dark hair loose now and flowing down nearly to his hands. His shoulders were just above hers and broader, making her look petite and lovely against the backdrop of him. Their eyes met in the mirror. Robin knew he saw what she saw, and if she hadn't been overcome by the urge for him to enter her, she might have been overwhelmed with sadness. What would her life be without him? What would their lives be like without each other?

But that was not what they discussed late that night as they lay in each other's arms.

"Your mom looked really good today. Happy, don't you think? I know she's been lonely since you've been at Binghamton."

"Well, sober, for sure," Robin answered.

"Why do you always bring that up?"

"You don't know how it was." Robin eased a bit out of his embrace. Why was he always such a champion of Mom? And why did that bother her so much? "You weren't around when she could barely make it across the room."

"Time to move on, babe. It's been four years. Your mom is so sweet and could really use your full support. The past is the past."

"And what other platitudes are you planning to throw at me? You also weren't around the thousand times she started drinking again—fell off the proverbial wagon."

"A thousand?"

Robin knew how much Matthew hated any sort of exaggeration. "Yes! A thousand." She fully extracted herself from him and was about to leave the bed when he pulled her back down.

"Oh, no, you don't," he said. They wrestled—her angry at first until he subdued her into laughter.

"I hate you," she said repeatedly until he kissed her so many times and so gently that he subdued her into love. "Okay. Okay. I love you. Now, can we go to sleep?"

Within moments, Matthew was breathing deeply beside her while Robin stared at the dark ceiling, feeling guilty and wondering if she'd ever get to the point where she would trust—could and should trust—Mom's sobriety.

It was the next day when Matthew and Robin were perusing the aisles of the local Ace Hardware—a pastime that Matthew loved—when he grabbed her hand and said, "I know what your mom needs. Look." He pointed at the end of the aisle, where there was a pen on the floor and a heat lamp and straw.

"A bunny?"

"No. Those aren't bunnies. Baby ducks. Didn't you say your mom loves ducks? What a nice Easter present ducks would be."

"Well, everyone loves ducks."

And sure enough, as they got closer, Robin could clearly see the adorable little puffs of brown and yellow. "Baby domestic Rouens."

"Your mom has that pond right outside the patio of her new apartment."

"True." Robin bent over the enclosure, and the next thing she knew—as if preordained—four little ducks scooted into her hands.

*A*uthor Note: Many, many years ago, I bought my mother four baby ducks. I can't remember what possessed me to do so, but the story that follows is one of my most cherished bird encounters. It involves thievery, the police, break-ins, and a chase scene!

Chapter 19: Seasonal Monogamy

Matthew and Robin sat on Mom's patio and watched the four ducks poke their beaks through the grass of the lawn between the patio and the edge of the pond. Mom sat on the grass among her duck children and smiled at their antics.

"I still don't know what possessed you two to bring me ducks." She said this with joy—something that Robin didn't often hear in Mom's voice.

"Easter. Ducks. Pond. It just made sense," said Matthew.

Robin reached out and squeezed his hand. It had been only a little over a week since they'd bought the ducklings, and already they were losing their baby-duck appearance—they'd easily doubled in size. Mom had named them Jenny, Joyce, Fred, and Harry, even though they were practically identical, and she couldn't tell them apart.

"Come. It's getting late," said Mom. "Let's go in and eat." As she got to her feet, all four ducklings peeped with anticipation. "Jenny-Joyce-Fred-Harry," she said as if they were one word, "time for dinner."

With a chorus of baby quacks, all four ducklings scurried around her feet and followed her into the house, with Matthew and Robin close behind. The ducklings went immediately to the enclosure Mom had made in the corner of her tiny kitchen. After they were rewarded with dinner, Mom locked them up, where they seemed totally content to eat before settling down for a nap under the heat lamp.

"They really are good ducks," said Mom as she passed Robin a bowl of salad for the table. "I'm probably the only forty-eight-year-old woman in Syracuse with four baby ducks in her kitchen. If that doesn't make me special, I don't know what will!"

T he next couple of months went by way too fast for Robin. Going to veterinary college had been a dream since she was seventeen, having decided that becoming an ornithologist was really not a career on its own and certainly something she could specialize in once she received her DVM. But as summer reached its peak and simmered toward fall, she dreaded more and more splitting with Matthew. She'd even considered trying to transfer to a school closer to Boston. She might have looked into it more thoroughly if it weren't for the fact that she refused to be that girl who followed a man. Not to mention that she'd been accepted at Cornell—the second-highest-rated veterinary college in the country. She was also unwilling to give up the significant scholarship she'd received. Her interest in ornithology had secured the scholarship, no doubt from the stories of Quentin and Maxine that she'd weaved into her essay.

Matthew and Robin visited Mom again in mid-August, one week before Robin was due to leave. The three of them sat on Mom's patio, enjoying the last warmth of the day. Matthew and Robin sipped glasses of wine, while Mom seemed content with her lemon La Croix. The sun was growing big on the horizon, turning deep orange, the colors shimmering off the pond. They sat in silence, watching the four ducks nearby on the grass.

Jenny, Joyce, Fred, and Harry were now fully feathered, and as it turned out, two of the young ducks were male, and two were female. They'd grown perfectly into their given names, Fred being the largest, with impressive blue-black feathers curling up from his tail and a deepgreen head. Joyce had definitely taken note of his handsomeness, making it obvious that their young friendship had taken a romantic twist. Likewise with Harry and Jenny. The two of them sat slightly away from Joyce and Fred, preening each other in a rather sexual manner. Robin felt the wonderful tingle of desire, watching the young lovers. The ducks gently ran their beaks deep into each other's feathers, making Robin glad she'd be going home to Matthew's apartment, where they could work on their own preening skills.

The young ducks had permanently moved outside. They spent a lot of their time with Mom when she was on her patio or working in her small garden. They always roosted near her back sliding glass door—the four of them in a tight feathered huddle under Mom's hydrangea bush. During the day, they were spending more and more time with the wild mallards that already occupied the pond. It was funny to see them swimming with the mallards, because their coloration was very similar, but they were already larger than all the other ducks—looking like overgrown teenagers trying to keep up with the cool adults.

"You know," said Mom, "I really think that both Joyce and Jenny wanted Fred. Jenny, sadly, had to settle."

"Poor Henry. Seconds," said Matthew.

"He looks happy enough," said Robin, still thinking of how Matthew would feel as she preened him this evening—as he hopefully preened her in return.

Late that night, Robin ran a finger through Matthew's hair. She used her right index finger like she was drawing pictures on his skull. He didn't seem to mind at all.

"Do you know," she asked, "that most swans and geese mate for life?" She didn't wait for an answer. "Most ducks practice seasonal monogamy."

"Seasonal monogamy? I like the sound of that."

She dug her fingernail a bit deeper into his scalp. He laughed.

"If a duck loses his or her mate, say because of a hunter, they will generally remate quickly. But... depending on the timing, their lives and productivity are greatly decreased. Even when they are remated, their mortality rate increases."

"Hmm." He turned to her and gathered her in his arms. He kissed her hard and then yawned with fatigue. Then he closed his eyes.

Even though she knew he was ready to go to sleep, she continued, "What do you think of marriage?"

His closed eyes opened to a tiny slit.

"If we got married, then we wouldn't be able to just forget about each other when we're so far apart."

"I'm not going to forget about you. No matter what."

"You say that, but once I'm outta sight, who knows? You know the saying: outta sight, outta mind. If we were married, we'd have all that legal stuff to have to deal with if the distance made us want to call it quits."

He laughed again and reclosed his eyes.

"You can't just laugh every time I say something rather than having a real discussion."

To Robin's dismay, he chuckled softly, released her, turned over, and fell asleep.

Author Note: When I was doing my research on the mating habits of waterfowl, I ran across the term "seasonal monogamy." What a great phrase! And what a great title for a future novel I've yet to write. It's so wonderful when two short words can conjure an entire story.

Chapter 20: Crazy, Sexy Duck Lady and the Keystone Cops

It was late October when Mom called. Robin was studying for her first big examination. She was in a cubicle at the Cornell Veterinary Library and had to step outside for fear others would hear Mom ranting on the phone.

"Then after they'd chased all the wild ducks from the pond, Jenny-Joyce-Fred-Harry were left all alone because, of course, they are just too chunky to fly away."

"How did they manage that?"

"They brought in a little boat. Had a gun, which I certainly hope they were shooting in the air. That's what Milly said. I was at work when all this was happening." Milly was Mom's neighbor. "And there's Jenny sitting on a nest of eggs even though it's late fall. And poor Henry beside himself, trying to protect her. Milly was crying when she told me about it."

Robin wrapped her coat tighter around her neck and wished she'd brought a scarf. Mom was talking pretty much in one continuous stream, but somehow Robin was mainly following.

"Then it got so cold this week. Did it get cold there? So cold, so fast. I guess poor Fred was out in the water. The other morning one of the other tenants saw Fred stuck in the ice. You know, in a thin sheet that froze so fast it got him stuck. Well, of course, as soon as it warmed a bit, he got himself right out. It's not like I was ignoring the problem. I'm not a bad duck mom. You know I've been looking for a place for them to go. Like a farm. I just found a place that will take them. The electric plant has a pond next to their building that they keep from freezing all winter. They have hundreds of ducks. I had no idea the apartment management had decided there was too much duck poop and were going to chase all the wild ducks off. If only they'd told me."

Robin stomped her feet and considered stepping back into the building. She could just imagine her feet getting stuck on the sidewalk—it felt that cold. Matthew and she really hadn't thought this duck thing through. Somehow, they hadn't considered winter and the fact that domestic ducks couldn't fly more than a few yards.

"Well, this man, the one who saw Fred in the ice, complained to the office, and before I even had a chance to do anything, they came and stole my ducks!"

"What?" asked Robin. "What do you mean, 'stole'?"

"Stolen! All except Jenny, because she was in the bushes on her eggs. Now she's freaking out and has left the nest. She's swimming all over the pond, calling for her friends—calling for Henry. She won't come to shore. Won't come to me. It's breaking my heart."

"But where are the other three?"

"I just finally found out where they took them. They're locked in an empty apartment they're remodeling. I've called the police. They should be here any moment."

"Wait. What? The police?"

"I can hear them quacking, and I see their little feet from under the door."

"But the police? Can't you just get them to let them out?"

"No. They said I couldn't have them back because I let Fred get frozen to the lake. All this stuff happened while I was at work. How was I supposed to know it would get so cold? I told them I had a place for them to go, but they just wouldn't listen. And now the office is closed, and it's Friday, so they won't be back until Monday."

There was a pause in her tirade. Robin wasn't sure whether she was just finally taking a breath, or the call dropped. Robin pictured the three ducks running around an empty apartment, quacking and pooping in a panic. "Mom?"

"I've got to go. They're here."

"Wait. Who's there? The police? Hold on. Is this really a good idea?" But all she heard was silence. Robin pulled her phone away from her ear and looked at the screen. Mom had ended the call. Robin checked the time. It was 5:36 and nearly fully dark. Matthew was due to be there by seven. It would be the first time they'd had a chance to see each other since the semester began. She needed a long shower and some serious time spent with her tweezer and razor. She went back into the library, grabbed her things, and called him as she walked through campus toward her apartment. He picked up on the third ring.

"My ETA is 7:40. Sorry. Got a late start." He sounded hollow and far away through the Bluetooth of his car.

"Boy, have I got a duck story for you."

It was hours later, after she and Matthew had eaten dinner and after they'd had slightly awkward but ultimately hot sex, when Robin was finally able to get a hold of Mom.

"It's nights like these," said Mom, "that I miss drinking the most." She laughed after she said this, which Robin thought was a good sign.

"It's nice that you can joke about that."

"Who's joking? So anyway... the police officers were so nice. Especially Frank. Did I tell you his name was Frank? When no one answered the emergency number for management, Frank said he was going to bust the door down. Joyce-Fred-Harry were in full panic mode, hearing my voice from outside the door. He was all poised to literally kick the door down when his partner—kind of a boring fellow—stepped right over, slipped in some kind of card thingy, and opened the door. You should have seen the three of us trying to corral Joyce-Fred-Harry. Like the Keystone Cops. But finally, each one of us had a duck. We put them right in the back of my car."

"And Jenny?"

"Jenny was nowhere to be found. My poor girl has either wandered off in her despair or was just hiding in the dark somewhere."

"Bet she shows up tomorrow." Robin yawned. She couldn't help it. She was exhausted.

Matthew sighed in his sleep next to her. She always loved the way he sighed in his sleep, as if he were having a beautiful dream. It must be wonderful to sleep so trouble free.

"I hope so. Frank and the other officer escorted me right to the electric company. Joyce-Fred-Harry waddled off right into the water. Even in the dark, we could see them make their way to the other ducks. I hope they make friends fast. Boy, what a night it's been."

Robin yawned again. "Let me know about Jenny tomorrow, okay?"

"Sure, honey. You sleep tight. Love you."

"Love you too."

"Oh, and by the way, Frank gave me his number. Says he wants to know how it turns out with Jenny and the others, but I think he likes me."

"Who wouldn't like a crazy, sexy duck lady?" Robin switched off the light on her nightstand. "Night, Duck Lady."

She ended the call, slipped fully under the covers, and turned her body so that it was nestled into Matthew's back. He sighed. Robin snuggled yet closer and sighed in return.

Author Note: Remember that all the bird stories in Early Bird *are true. My mother really did call the cops. My memory tells me that the officers actually knocked down the door. Since this happened over forty years ago and my mother is no longer with us to verify, I decided that*

breaking the door was just too unbelievable, thus a true example of truth being stranger than fiction.

Chapter 21: Dance of the Duck

It was late Sunday afternoon when Robin pulled into Mom's parking lot. Matthew was right behind her in his own car. The plan was for him to drive back to Boston directly from Syracuse. But first they had an important task.

Mom hugged Robin nearly to the point of pain just as soon as she opened the apartment door. She did the same to Matthew. "Thank you. Thank you both so much for driving all the way here."

"Come on," said Matthew. "You don't need to thank us." He rubbed at his arm. "You've got quite an embrace there. Like a sumo wrestler or something. We are, after all, the ones who got you into this mess by bringing you Jenny-Joyce-Fred-Harry."

They stepped into the apartment.

"Wow, you said that just like Mom."

"What? Jenny-Joyce-Fred-Harry? You can't say that?"

Robin shook her head and laughed.

"Come on. You can do it. Say it."

"No. I can't. You know my tongue won't work like that."

He grabbed her by the shoulders and pretended to give her a good shaking. "Say it. Say it!"

Mom began to laugh. Robin flushed with pleasure. They'd had a wonderful weekend. The best in a long while. Maybe there was something to the distance-making-the-heart-grow-fonder cliché.

He spun her from the small foyer into Mom's living room. "Say it."

"Jenny-oyce-Fedry. Wait. No. Enny-Joyce-Fredhy."

Mom was laughing so hard she had to sit down.

"I can't do it. I just can't."

He released her shoulders and hugged her to his chest. "And that, Robin Aletta Byrd," he whispered into her ear, "is why I love you."

"You two are so cute together," said Mom. "When are you going to get married?"

"Shut up, Mom."

And of course, Matthew just laughed.

"Come. Let's eat before we try to catch her."

While Matthew was helping Mom get the food to the table, Robin watched Jenny through the glass of the patio door. It was late afternoon, the sun low in the sky. The duck was near the shore, pacing slowly, looking as distraught as a duck could look.

"She's totally stopped going in the water," said Mom.

"Who knew a duck could look so sad. And her eggs?"

"They are out there in the nest. Seven of them. I went out and tried to get her interested again, but it just didn't happen. I'd imagine they're all quite rotten by now."

They ate the tuna casserole of Robin's childhood—thick and salty with Campbell's Cream of Mushroom soup and slices of green olives, topped with a thick layer of crumbled Ruffles potato chips. A murderous comfort food. A happy belly while you slowly died. Even though it was getting late, both Robin and Matthew took seconds. The dinner conversation consisted primarily of strategizing. By the time Matthew wiped his mouth and threw his napkin onto his plate—an act Robin disliked, especially when that napkin was made of linen—they had a perfect plan.

Jenny eyed them warily.

"Come here, Jenny, Jenny."

"Sweet Jenny."

"Duck. Duck. Cute little duck."

"You want some corn? I have corn."

She cocked her head and quacked softly at their kind words, but as soon as they approached, she waddled quickly away. Their strategy of simply outnumbering her and slowing her down with kindness wasn't working. After ten minutes of sticking to the plan, slowly, like a dance, the pace increased.

"Go that way."

"She's faking to the right."

"No, you don't!"

"Dammit!"

"Come here, you stupid duck!"

Matthew exploded into a run. Jenny threw out her wings and half waddled, half flew just out of his reach. She stopped three feet away. Matthew launched his body like an Ohio State first-string tackle but came up empty as Jenny flapped to his left. She landed between Mom and Robin with a series of loud quacks.

"I think she's laughing at you."

Matthew sat on the grass, catching his breath. "Stupid duck. I'm beginning to really regret all that tuna and noodles."

"Oh, Jenny," said Mom. "Don't you remember how you used to follow me everywhere?"

Jenny gave Mom a soft quack, shook out her feathers, and brought them all back in neat alignment.

"Guess we all end up leaving the nest at some point," said Robin.

As if taking a bow, Matthew spread out his arms. Jenny took a step toward Robin. In one fluid ballerina movement, Robin scooped her up.

Mom clapped her hands together. "Bravo!"

Jenny quacked in response.

Matthew completed his bow.

It was nearly dark by the time they pulled into the parking lot of the electric company. The pond was larger than the one at Mom's and originated at the building. Water poured from a huge brass pipe protruding from the exterior wall. It cascaded into a series of increasingly larger square concrete rectangles that stair-stepped down. The final largest one emptied into the pond in an impressive flow. Robin wondered if there was an interior twin water feature within the building. It must use an extraordinary amount of electricity. "Our utilities at work," said Robin. "I guess that's what keeps the pond from freezing."

"That and all the moving duck legs," said Matthew. Clustered in the center of the pond were hundreds of ducks, all of them looking identical from this distance, pulsating as a unit. Soft quacks reached their ears. Every few seconds, the quacking increased in volume only to fade out to a murmur.

"Oh my," said Mom. "How is Jenny ever going to find them?"

The closer they got to the water's edge, the harder Jenny struggled in Robin's arms.

"Here goes nothing."

Robin bent down and placed Jenny gently on the ground. She immediately started in with a loud, persistent *quack, quack, quack*. She hit the water quacking and paddled toward the mass of fowl. Matthew, Mom, and Robin looked on in the fading light. The water was almost copper, with soft ripples. Jenny's quacking dominated the sounds of falling water, the nearby highway traffic, and the chatter of hundreds of ducks settling in for the night.

To Robin's amazement, the mass of duck moved and split. Within moments, three ducks broke free from the others. What surely must have been Joyce-Fred-Harry paddled toward Jenny. All four ducks quacked with increasing intensity.

As they grew near, Jenny-Joyce-Fred-Harry raised their bodies as if walking on water, their necks up and their wings stretched out in welcome. The four became united in necks and wings and beaks and soft quacks. They swam in tiny circles. Tears ran down Robin's cheeks. She glanced at Mom, who was crying too. Matthew wiped at his eyes and took Robin's hand. Robin reached for Mom's hand. The three of them watched the four young ducks—silhouettes against the copper water—until they moved as one and joined the others.

Author Note: I've thought about those four ducks over the years. I'd like to think they stayed bonded, living out their lives in harmony with all the other ducks. I imagine the employees of the electric company sharing crumbs from their lunches and fawning over all the sweet little baby ducks that were sure to follow. Perhaps their great-great-great-great-grandducks are still paddling around under the shade of the electric company building.

Chapter 22: Slices of Quince

R obin gently turned the cockatoo upside down and stroked his under-feathers. He didn't seem to mind, so she carefully pulled out his left wing and inspected the lesion. The ulceration was healing well. "Look at you, buddy." She turned him back over and allowed him to claw his way up her arm. "You must be feeling better. Shall we keep up the treatment for another week?"

He bobbed his entire body in agreement.

"Excellent." Robin moved her arm so that Caesar could transfer to Mr. Kiley's. Caesar made his way to Mr. Kiley's shoulder and nibbled on his owner's impressive earlobes.

Mr. Kiley rubbed the parrot's head and said, "I used to have normal-sized ears until this guy became part of my life."

Robin laughed. Caesar looked at her and laughed too. The laugh was loud and feminine. She assumed it was the laugh of Mr. Riley's departed wife.

"He's been with you thirty years now?"

"Yup. Bought him from a guy named Baretta."

Caesar and Mr. Kiley laughed heartily, letting Robin know it was a joke. She laughed but didn't get it. She made a mental note to google Baretta when she got the chance.

Caesar was one of the first birds Robin had treated when she opened her avian veterinarian practice. She'd struggled with her decision to stay in Ithaca, knowing that her practice might be more successful in a bigger city, but in the end, the uniqueness of Ithaca had won her over. It turned out there was a large number of exotic pet birds kept in the area and an even greater number of individuals keeping chickens, ducks, geese, and turkeys. Ithacans were quite passionate about their birds, whether for companionship, eggs, or meat. In the two years since she'd opened her doors, she'd also formed a nice network with local bird rehabilitators and surrounding area zoos—traveling as far as Buffalo or Binghamton to call on a sick bird. Having the name of Dr. Byrd didn't hurt. Her reputation as the area's avian expert was taking off. She was just able to make her student loan payments and afford an occasional treat, such as an extra shot of espresso at Collegetown Bagels.

"Well, Mr. Kiley, he looks really good. I'd say unless you have a concern, just keep up the medication for one more week, and I'll see him in six months. Sound good?"

Caesar bobbed his body.

"What he said," answered Mr. Kiley.

As Robin escorted Mr. Kiley and the parrot back out into the reception area, she heard her vet tech, Brenda, say into the phone, "I'm sorry, Dr. Byrd's practice is exclusively birds. I'd be glad to give you Dr. Stewart's number. He's only a mile from our office."

Brenda said that at least three times a day. Brenda had been with Robin since she opened her doors. They'd learned together, Brenda fresh with her vet tech degree and the ink still wet on Robin's veterinary license. Brenda was dressed especially oddly in what looked like a made-over light-blue prom dress cut into a long shirt, which she wore over pink leggings. Her Doc Martins seemed totally out of place, especially with her ponytail positioned like a unicorn's horn and her eye makeup extra blue and glittery.

Brenda caught Robin's eye and rolled her own. "I'm sorry you feel that way. It's really nothing against you or Pumpkin. You want a vet who specializes in cats, right? Dr. Stewart is brilliant when it comes to kitties."

While it wouldn't kill Robin to treat dogs or cats, she knew that might not be true for a stressed bird being brought into an office full of barking dogs and mewing cats. The only exception she'd made was an occasional turtle or lizard.

After Mr. Kiley left, Brenda and Robin sat outside, enjoying the shade of the front porch and eating their lunch. Most recently a dental practice, the clinic was a small, renovated house on Green Street, just a few blocks from Ithaca Commons and a mile from Cornell. Robin was extremely lucky the old dentist had dropped dead of a heart attack. His family was eager for a quick sale and had given her a heck of a deal. She rented the two apartments on the second floor to Cornell veterinary students. The income just about covered the mortgage. Her situation might have been too good to be true if she weren't over four hundred thousand dollars in debt with student loans, the building's mortgage, and the financing of the four-wheel-drive truck she needed to negotiate the steep, snowy streets of Ithaca and the surrounding area.

"Oh, it's already so hot," said Brenda, fanning herself with her napkin. "Here it's not even June."

"Stop right there. Never complain about heat and sun." Robin took a large bite of her tuna fish sandwich and chewed just enough to be able to say, "Have you forgotten already how minus five degrees feels?"

"Oh, I like it cold. The colder the better."

Robin reached for her water bottle. The bread was the healthy kind that was so popular in Ithaca—good for you if you didn't choke. "You're certainly living in the right—"

"Dr. Byrd?"

Robin looked up. A woman was coming up the porch steps, carrying one of the biggest great horned owls Robin had ever seen. Based on the bird's size, she thought it must be female. The woman cradled her like a football under one arm and supported the rest of her with the other. The bulk of the bird was swaddled in what looked like a jacket or shirt because sleeves fell from either side rather than wings. "A pet owl?" Robin whispered.

She must have said it louder than intended because Brenda answered, "That's so cool. I want a pet owl."

And the woman responded, "No. Not a pet."

The bird was gorgeous.

The owl swiveled her head this way and that. Her huge yellow eyes found Robin, who had stood. Robin saw and felt the bird's anger, fear, and pain. Her tuft feathers—giving the bird its name, "horned" owl—went up and then back down. She moved as if to bite her companion, her beak opening then closing slowly. *Not worth the effort,* she seemed to be thinking. The disc feathers surrounding her eyes and beak were creamy and fluffy and gave her that quintessential look of wisdom.

"Look at those eyes," said Brenda. "Like slices of quince."

The woman gave Brenda a confused look before turning back to Robin. "I was out hiking near Taughannock Falls and found him. He's hurt. He can barely fly. Maybe his wing is broken."

"She, by the look of her," said Robin. "Here." Robin opened the clinic door. "Bring her in."

Robin knew the bird was in bad shape. A non-critically ill wild great horned owl would never put up with being carried like a naughty toddler. The combination of powerful wings and beak along with up to five hundred pounds per square inch of talon strength would make it impossible to capture and carry a less sick owl.

"Put her here," Robin said, indicating the metal table in examination room one.

Brenda was ready with the midazolam to sedate the bird, which she administered quickly and efficiently. Within moments, the bird was relaxed enough for Robin to gently extend the wings and check for fractures. The woman stood in the corner, biting the nail of her right thumb and jiggling one of her feet hard enough for Robin to notice.

It didn't take long to locate the problem. On the underside of the bird's left wing was a wound. It was high up in the wing pit, nearly to the breast. The wound was raw, round, and reddish black with infection.

"It appears she was shot," said Robin.

"Shot? Who would do such a terrible thing to such a stunning creature?"

Robin just shook her head. "It's illegal to shoot a predatory bird. But people do it. Maybe they thought she was eating their chickens. Maybe for the sport." Robin stroked the bird's feathers. "Owls have soft, fluffy feathers that make their flight nearly silent," she whispered. "Unlike the noisy but swift flight of a hawk, owls are slow and stealthy." Robin's fingers got lost in the feathers. "Most animals never hear them coming. Just like this beautiful girl." Robin moved closer so that her face was nearly to the owl's breast. She was tempted to nuzzle the feathers with her nose. "You're so magnificent. I bet you never heard the bullet until it was too late. How could anyone not see the beauty of your existence?"

A small noise pulled Robin's attention away from the bird. She glanced up and saw that tears were running down Brenda's cheeks—blue glitter was making its way down her face.

"Such an elegant fowl," said Brenda.

Robin had learned to ignore most of Brenda's random utterances, but with that, she sighed, recognizing the reference to Edward Lear's poem. She let the fact that owls weren't fowl go. "Let's try to help you dance by the light of the moon," she whispered to the owl. She put on a grim smile, straightened, and turned to the woman who'd brought the bird in. "I'm going to clean the wound and put her on IV fluids and antibiotics. Then—" Her fingers lingered in the bird's soft down. "Well, we'll just have to see."

The woman nodded. "She has such magnificent eyes. I'm an optometrist, you see, so I've looked at a lot of eyes. But these... It's as if they are looking right into... well, not my soul, because that's just too cliché. More like my beating heart."

"Like she wants to reach in and rip it out," said Brenda.

As if on cue, the light sedation failed just enough that the bird swiveled her head, her gaze hitting each of them before the yellow globes disappeared once again under the creamy white lids.

Author Note: In this true-life owl encounter, I was the one who was walking in the woods that day. I was alone and heard a crashing noise. I saw the incredible bird struggling to escape my approach. Try as she might, she could not fly more than a few feet. I approached slowly. Hesitant to grab her with my bare hands, I took off my shirt and tossed it over her. Fortunately, I had on a camisole, so I didn't have to walk home in my bra. I took her to our country vet, who was involved in local bird rehabilitation.

Chapter 23: Acceptance Is Stupid

Robin was exhausted, not just physically but in every aspect of her existence. "I'm too young to feel so old," she said to no one in particular.

The middle-aged Indian man who passed her on the sidewalk said something that sounded like "Amen to that."

Robin stopped, turned around, and called to him, "Seriously, do you ever wish you were really old so you would die soon and just get it over with?"

He stopped, turned her way, and cocked his head. He put his arms up in surrender. "Accept completely. That is all for which we should wish."

She stared at him a moment. "Well, that's just stupid." Robin turned and continued hiking up the steep hill toward her parked truck. The day had started poorly and continued to deteriorate since the owl.

Mom had called just as they finished cleaning and dressing the owl's wound and setting up the IV. For weeks, Robin had been nursing a growing suspicion that Mom was drinking again. The phone call pretty much confirmed it. Mom was way too happy, all over the place, and seemed to be slurring her words. They'd have to call a family meeting soon, if only Robin could figure out the family aspect of the meeting.

Dad was going through yet another divorce. His love life was such that he might well have been a celebrity. Every time Robin spoke with him, all he talked about was how the latest woman was royally screwing him. "All I have to do is bend over and expose my wallet" was one of his favorite—and way too frequent—sayings. Robin couldn't remember the last time he'd asked her how she was doing. He certainly didn't appear to care about how Mom might be.

Then there was Wren. The last Robin knew, her sister was eating grubs and hiking in the Amazon basin with some woman she'd met on Tinder. Robin had not heard from her in months. For all Robin knew, Wren could have been dragged off by an anaconda or succumbed to yellow fever with a little malaria mixed in.

The only one of her immediate family who seemed to have it together was Jay. He and Christina were expecting their first child in two months, but he'd just texted Robin an hour ago and told her there were complications with the pregnancy, and Christina had been put on bed rest. The last thing he needed was bad news about Mom.

"Acceptance is stupid," she said as she finally made it to the top of the hill and turned left toward her truck. Once she was behind the wheel, it took three tries to get the old truck going. *What's going to happen this winter when the temperature is subzero?*

She bit her lip while she drove through the crowded streets of Ithaca, making her way down the hill toward Newfield. Her indecision regarding the owl plagued her while she drove. The wound on the owl showed every indication of gangrene. The antibiotics were unlikely to help at that point. Amputation was really the only way to save the owl's life.

But what sort of life would that be? The owl was a wild, beautiful creature. Amputation would mean she'd spend the rest of her life in a cage. Euthanasia was the more humane choice. But to directly kill such a magnificent animal—it was something Robin would never get used to. She'd left the bird hooked up to pain meds, fluids, and antibiotics, and tried to toss its fate to the universe. If there was a god, the owl would be dead in the morning, allowing Robin her indecision.

By the time Robin reached the city limits, she was so angry that she hit the steering wheel in frustration. She was angry with the hunter who'd put her in that position. She was angry with the optometrist for finding the bird and bringing her in. She was angry with herself for being so angry. She was apparently angry at life itself.

She parked on the street in front of where she called home—a tiny blue house on a tree-lined street. It would have been wonderful to live in Ithaca, but the rent was way more than she could presently afford.

As she entered the side door of the bottom floor she rented, her cell phone pinged. Without giving the screen a glance, she pulled it out of her pocket, turned off the sound, and laid it face down on the kitchen counter with a notable thud. The world—her world—would not end if she unplugged. She glanced at the clock on the microwave. "I'm not looking at you for at least an hour," she told the phone.

Benjamin called from the living room.

"I'm not talking to you," Robin said, stepping into the room and finding him making his way across the couch like a tiny soldier. Her anger began to lessen. She doubted she'd ever stop being anything but amused every time she saw him. Bright yellow and wingless, he looked more like a fuzzy popsicle than a budgie. He'd sustained massive injuries after being caught in netting. His family hadn't wanted to pay the cost of treatment and told her to euthanize him, but she just couldn't do it. That had been a year ago, and the little guy was hilarious.

She went to him and let the little budgie climb onto her finger and then her hand. She sat on the couch, and as he made his way up her arm and onto her shoulder, she began to cry. At first, it was just a little thing—just a few stupid tears filling up the spaces between her eyelids. Having nowhere else to go, they trickled down her cheeks. She began to hiccup with misery, gulping in air and snorting out sorrow. So great was her grief that Benjamin abandoned her, pulling out what was left of his wings, dropping to the couch, and walking away in apparent disgust.

At some point later, she felt Matthew's fingers on her shoulders. Her eyes opened, and it was nearly dark. Hours had gone by. She sat up slightly, seeing his face in the fairytale light that streamed through the window from the setting sun.

"Oh, Matthew," she said and burst into tears all over again. He held her tightly until all the outside light had left the room. Benjamin made his way to them and sat in the small space their bodies made—under their chins and above their chests.

"You took the test today, didn't you?" he asked.

She nodded. She couldn't say the words, so he did.

"It was negative." He sighed so deeply it caused Benjamin to squawk. "Fucking IVF."

*A*uthor Note: *The quote by Eckhart Tolle, "Whatever the present moment contains, accept it as if you had chosen it," is easier to say than to put into practice. This is especially true for the young. If you're lucky, part of getting old enough to have the right to feel old is realizing how simple it is to sigh at whatever comes along and say, "It is what it is." So while the title of this chapter is Acceptance Is Stupid, that's not at all what I believe. By accepting each moment as if you had chosen it, you are embracing and truly living that moment. And what better way to live your life than to live it in the moment of your choice?*

Chapter 24: The Problem with Whales

As Robin entered the front door of her practice the next morning, she took one look at Brenda and knew all was not well with the owl. "Please be dead," Robin whispered.

"She's not," said Brenda.

Robin wished for the thousandth time that she could shake her habit of speaking rather than thinking. She clamped her mouth shut, hung her purse on the hook in her office, and went to the recovery room. She glanced in the kennel at the pile of disheveled feathers moving up and down, turned around, and went back to her office. After shutting the door, she took out her cell phone and called her friend at Cornell. The call was quick and to the point. She looked at the time on her phone, deciding she would allow three more minutes of feeling sorry for herself. She teared up but not to the point that it might dislodge mascara.

She would try again. As horrific as the IVF treatments had been—her mood swings, the ugly bruises, the pain, and the cost—it was a course they were not ready to give up on. Having a baby was the main reason they'd bothered to get married. Sinfully cohabitating would have been fine otherwise. Throw a child into the mix, and marriage just seemed the way to go.

Robin had watched Matthew interact with his niece and nephews over the years. She'd seen the joy on his face. He wanted this more than she did, and it broke her heart that she was failing him. Or more accurately, her stupid body was failing them both. Four years into trying, hiding their aching secret—only her mother knew—she was feeling the fatigue, the hopelessness, and the fear. Would he leave her for more fertile ground? Was she so insecure that this thought actually danced about in her head? What kind of relationship—what kind of marriage—was that?

Robin glanced at her cell phone. Her three minutes were up. She sighed, shook her head as if she were ridding herself of flies, got up, and left her office.

Brenda was there, as ready as always.

"Let's do this thing," Robin said, and the two of them headed for the recovery room.

T he waters had been relatively smooth until they'd rounded the tip of Cape Cod. The boat was now in open sea and crowded with so many people eager to see a whale. They'd been bouncing around for nearly an hour, and Robin was getting tired. It had been years since she'd been to the cape. Years since she and Matthew had taken a vacation of any sort. "We'd better do it now, while we have the chance," he'd said, convincing her to close the practice for a long, much-needed week away.

Robin planted her feet farther apart and held on to the rail. Matthew stood near, his hand tightly on her shoulder as if his only desire were to keep her upright. Her hair blew across her face and then straight back.

"I'll never let go. I'll never let go," said Matthew into her ear.

She peered out at the roiling waters. Here she was, nearly thirty-two and had yet to see a whale—not even in a zoo or an aquarium. "I don't think we're going to see one," Robin said for the third time.

"We don't need to. I'm looking at one right now," he said for the third time.

"It's not getting any funnier."

"Are you sure?"

"I may have to go sit dow—"

The water heaved up. Not more than thirty yards away, a whale emerged. Up it went, until its entire body was out, and then down. The splash was impressive, and before Robin had the chance to wipe at her face, she was shoved forward, her hard, round belly pressed against the metal railing.

"Hey!" said Matthew. "Pregnant woman here!"

Robin felt the boat tip downward. All the passengers had run in one great mass to their side of the boat. The pressure grew against her back. The metal dug into her tummy. She feared for her unborn child. She feared the boat might capsize. The whale breached again, this time even closer, which brought the mass to near hysteria. Matthew managed to get fully behind her and shove the people off.

"Can't you see she's pregnant? It's a goddamn whale! Not the second coming. Get away from her!" He shoved at the mob and pulled on her arm until she was safely away from the rail.

The throng filled in the gap, clueless to what they had done.

Once to safety, Robin bent over her baby, placing her hands on her thighs, and panted. "That's how people get trampled."

"Are you okay?"

"I think so."

"Unbelievable."

Later on, when the boat was heading back to the dock, the incident seemed rather funny. She was almost dry and starting to warm up. They were sitting inside the open cabin at a little metal table. Matthew was sipping a beer, and Robin was drinking hot chocolate. She was sitting sideways on the bench because her stomach wouldn't fit. She pushed gently on her belly, wanting more than anything to feel movement.

"Maybe a whale watch was not the best idea," she said.

"You think?"

"Dr. Byrd?"

Robin looked up. The woman looked familiar, but Robin couldn't quite place her.

"Remember me? I'm the one who brought in the great horned owl that had been shot. A couple of years ago? The optometrist."

"Of course." Robin tried to get up, but the woman quickly waved her down.

"May I?" she asked, indicating the space on the bench next to Matthew.

"Please," said Matthew, sliding over a bit.

Robin had no idea what the woman's name was and was relieved when she said, "I'm sure you don't remember my name. I'm Stacey. Stacey Moran."

"This is Matthew, my husband."

They made their hellos.

"I can't believe I ran into you here," said Stacey.

"Did you? Were you one of the ones who ran into her?" asked Matthew. He narrowed his eyes, but his mouth gave him away.

Robin laughed. "Ignore him." She briefly recounted the story for Stacey.

"Oh my! I hope it wasn't me. When are you due?"

"Three and a half weeks."

"First?"

Robin nodded.

"Well, I won't keep you, but I just wanted to tell you again how grateful I am for your efforts in trying to save that poor—"

"Yes." Robin was suddenly sad. Euthanizing that beautiful creature had been one of the hardest things she had ever done. "The infection was just too advanced."

"But what I wanted to tell you," said Stacey, quickly waving at the air as if to push away the sadness, "was that I had a patient just last week who is doing research on retinal dystrophies such as retinitis pigmentosa. I guess he's making great progress. We got to talking, and it turns out he's using our owl! *Our* actual owl's eyes. I guess owl rods are large, and they have a lot of them. A perfect source for research."

Robin smiled and nodded. Of course, she knew this.

"I know you must have called him. But it's such a coincidence that he came to me for an eye exam. As if it were meant to be. At the time, her death seemed so tragic and pointless. It's just nice that her death had a purpose, you know?"

Robin felt the baby roll its tiny fist across the interior wall of her abdomen—the first stirrings since Robin had been pinned against the rail. She placed her hand on her belly. The baby answered by pushing against her palm. Robin's smile widened. "I know. And thank you for bringing her to me. I agree. It felt so disheartening and pointless at the time. But as it turns out...Well, I guess it turns out that *pointless* is a rather silly word."

*A*uthor Note: *In the real-life version of this bird story, I remember being fascinated when the researcher at Syracuse University told me he was using great horned owl rods for his research, but I was absolutely amazed when I realized they were from my owl's eyes. My other "claim to fame" research-wise involved a chocolate oranda goldfish I loved that ended up with a tumor in its gill. I took it to the College of Veterinary Medicine at Ohio State University for surgery, which is a short story in itself. Ultimately, the tumor grew back, and when the goldfish died, the university wanted the tumor for research. It turned out to be a rare myxoma and ended up in the Smithsonian.*

Chapter 25: Best Intentions

Robin sprayed the Odor Eaters liberally into Mason's sneaker. She used so much that it dripped out when she turned the shoe upside down. She knew it was overkill, but his shoes seemed to stink up the entire house. He'd had smelly shoes since the very first time he'd placed his little feet within a pair. It didn't seem to matter if they were leather, synthetic, or cotton. And now that he was pushing eleven and nearing adolescence, it was bordering on a health hazard. Luckily, Ethan's feet were wondrously perfect. Even though he was eight years old, she wanted to put Ethan's toes in her mouth, as she had when he was a baby.

She moved on to the next pair, picking one up gingerly. Her cell phone squawked to life in her pocket, causing her to drop the shoe, more with relief than startlement. It took three loud macaw squawks before she managed to extract the phone and look at the screen. *Mom. Only Mom. Not a vet emergency, thank God.*

"Hi there," Robin said once she managed to get the device to her ear.

"I'm a grandma for the seventh time!"

The baby wasn't due for another three weeks. "Really? Is everything okay?"

"Wren and baby are doing wonderfully. I just WhatsApped them. A little girl. Finally, we have added a little girl to the mix."

It was true. Jay and Christina had four raucous boys. With her two, every family gathering was like a mini rugby game.

Robin sat down on the mudroom bench and sighed with relief. She'd only seen Wren once in the last ten years, and then only because she'd made the trip alone to Bolivia. It was a trek out to the small village Wren called home. Her sister had thrived as an Amazon woman. She was clothed in colorful local garb, her long dark hair braided and tied up in crazy loops around her head. Her skin was sandy dark with sun, her eyes bright and blue—she looked just like she'd stepped off the cover of an adventure romance novel. And she looked happy, as happy and content as Robin had ever seen her.

Wren was affiliated with the Bolivian Red Cross, and while never officially educated in medical care, she worked in pretty much every capacity within the small local medical clinic. While Robin had been there, she'd watched her sister hold a man while he died, pull a breech calf out of a cow that a local farmer had brought to the clinic, clean pounds and pounds of bedding and surgical equipment, administer medications and IV fluids, feed patients spoonful by spoonful, and even scrape tarantula legs off the clinic floor.

"They're still moving," said Wren as she lifted one up to show Robin. "I usually just scoot them back outside, but a lot of the locals just step on them." She frowned. "I wish I'd had time to stop the boy who smashed this one."

"Maybe next time he'll take your lead."

Wren smiled up at her. "It's the little things, you know? Just trying to make a difference." Wren had pretty much read the boy the riot act just moments after the squashing.

"I know. And it's not a little thing at all as far as the tarantulas are concerned."

In spite of their different responses to their often-difficult upbringing—and the totally different paths her brother and sister had taken from hers—it amazed Robin how similar the three of them were. Somehow, they each had keen and deep empathy for all creatures—no matter how creepy or venomous. It was just last year that Jay had carefully helped a slightly injured copperhead off the road after watching the car in front of him take off the tip of its tail. The hot turkey story was one of Jay's favorites to share—apparently having conveniently for-gotten his annoyance at the time. "My daddy saved a hot turkey once," was one of the first sentences her youngest nephew had said to her.

And now they had a new Byrd in the family. A little girl Byrd.

"Has she named her yet?" Robin asked Mom.

"Rain."

"Excuse me?"

"Her name is Rain."

Robin laughed. "Better than Drought, I guess."

Wren and Rain. It was perfect.

"Middle name?"

"Oh dear. I forgot to ask. Maybe Drop?"

Robin laughed. As much as Robin would love her boys to meet their aunt and now their little girl cousin, Matthew was concerned about dragging them through the jungles of Bolivia. She hoped to change his mind now that the baby was born. From what Robin and the rest of her family had managed to piece together, Wren had had an assortment of lovers over the years, the vast majority of them women. But unless this was immaculate conception or voodoo, Wren had been with at least one man.

As if Mom was reading her mind, she said, "She's dark, of course. And so very beautiful. I want so much to meet her."

Robin could hear the tears in Mom's voice. They both knew that unless Wren brought the baby home, Mom would never meet her. Though Mom had been sober now for more than eight years, her health was steadily declining. *Too little, too late* was the basic diagnosis. Or more accurately *too much, too long.*

"At least there's WhatsApp," Robin offered.

"True. When it works."

The back door flew open, causing Robin to nearly drop the phone.

"Mom! Mom!"

"Look what we found!"

She looked up at her sweaty boys—their dark hair tousled, their eyes aglow with delight. Matthew grinned from behind him. He, too, in spite of his recent gray hairs, looked like an excited boy.

"I'll call you back in a little bit," said Robin to Mom and ended the call.

"We saved it! We saved it before the owl could bite its head off too."

"It's an orphan. Its poor mom was killed. Her head was chopped clean off."

"Gruesome! Gory! And so cool!"

"Wait. Slow down," said Robin, standing up. "Found what?"

Matthew pulled his hands away from his body and presented to her what looked like nothing more than a child's stuffed toy. White and brown, the tiny creature was a powder puff with two insanely large dark eyes and a massive yellow beak. Robin took a step closer.

"You found this where?" she asked.

"On the ground, by a tree," said Ethan so loudly that the baby bird startled. "Its mama's head was gone! Lying right next to him on the ground. Mean ol' owl was looking down at us from the tree."

"Yes! Yes! The owl was just waiting to swoop down and pluck the baby's head off too. But we saved it just in time," said Mason. "Dad, let me hold him. Let me hold him."

Both boys tried to grab the chick from Matthew, who put his hands above his head. They laughed and jumped against their father's body.

"Give him to me!"

"No! Me! Me!"

Matthew twirled around with the boys in tow, the poor little bird held up like an offering.

Robin put up her hand to silence them. "Stop. Stop, all of you." She turned her hand over and gestured for Matthew to give her the bird. Once it was securely in her possession, she ruffled the soft white down on the top of its head. The chick closed its eyes with apparent relief.

"This, you silly men, is not an orphan. This is a baby barred owl. What you've actually done is called *kidnapping*."

Author Note: I'm nearing to the end of my list of remarkable bird stories. In fact, this baby owl story was borrowed from my brother. He was the one who was walking through the woods years ago and came across the grisly scene of a headless bird next to a creature he claims to have been nothing but fluff and big black eyes. I believe his memory has exaggerated the pure cuteness of this little animal, and I felt it necessary to add the beak to my description. Unfortunately, this occurred way before the ease of taking photos with a cell phone, so there is no documentation.

Chapter 26: Oggy Isn't Blue—He's a Happy Owl

"Kidnapping? What are you talking about?" asked Matthew. The boys looked at each other, their eyes growing wide.

Robin walked from the mudroom into the kitchen, her family trailing after her. "This little guy belongs to the 'mean ol' owl' up in the tree. Most likely the mom, but I bet if you'd looked around a little more carefully, you'd have found Dad nearby." The baby owl bobbed its head up and down as if agreeing with her. She stroked its fluffy neck. "You fell from your nest cavity, right?"

"But we saw the mom dead on the ground," insisted Matthew.

"That wasn't Mom. That was dinner."

"Dinner?" asked both boys.

"Yuck," added Mason.

"You mean the adult owl killed another bird to feed to this little guy?" asked Matthew. "Just dropped it near him?"

"Apparently. You're lucky its parents didn't attack you."

"He fell from his nest?" asked Ethan.

"Yup." Robin sat at the kitchen table and set the baby on one of the placemats.

Both boys ran over and gently petted the bird.

"We need to get you back to your parents," said Robin.

"Yeah. Before they call the cops!" Matthew added.

"I want to name him Oggy," said Ethan.

"He's not a cat," said Mason. "And he's not blue."

"I like the name Oggy."

"It's stupid."

"It is not."

"Oggy Owl is perfect," interjected Robin before it turned into a full-fledged battle. "Speaking of names, your aunt Wren had her baby today." She looked up at Matthew and smiled. "That was Mom on the phone. All is well."

Matthew squeezed her shoulder. He knew how worried she'd been about her sister. It seemed to Robin that she'd spent most if not all of her life worrying about Wren. It was a hard habit to break. After her trip to Bolivia, she was finally coming to realize that Wren was a brilliant, self-sufficient, all-grown-up woman who'd perhaps never deserved Robin's concern. But all that had fallen apart when Wren became pregnant.

"Boy or girl?" asked Matthew.

Robin's smile broadened. "Girl. Her name is Rain."

"Rain?" cried Mason. "Bet she's wet." Both boys laughed.

"Rain, rain, go away," sang Ethan.

The little owl, startled by the sudden verbal assault, clutched the placemat with its tiny talons and clicked its beak. Robin tried to soothe him with her touch. The clicking got louder. "Yes, I know. You are scared. We're going to get you home soon."

Matthew, apparently worried for the integrity of the placemat, gently extracted it from the baby's grasp. "Owls can pick up all sorts of things," he said. "Why didn't they just pick him up and put him back in the nest?"

"Predatory birds know instinctually that their talons are too strong. Too likely to kill the baby. They are weapons."

"Wow," said Ethan. "That's super cool."

"So I should go get out our extension ladder, I guess," said Matthew.

"Nope," said Robin. She couldn't help herself—she bent over and kissed the baby owl on the top of its head. "No one's getting on a ladder with two angry adult owls nearby. What we need is a strong wooden box, like that packing crate that's been sitting in the garage forever, and some nails."

They lined the wooden crate with pine straw and dry leaves. Robin held the crate securely while Matthew used his portable drill to screw the box in place on the side of the large oak near where the bird was found. They placed the nest box off the ground but not so high that they would be unable to peek in and check on Oggy.

"Screws will be more secure and easier to use than pounding nails," he'd explained to her.

Mom and Dad Owl observed silently from above.

Robin and Matthew stood back and studied their work. It took some time, but finally, Matthew spotted the nesting cavity, way up high, formed between a fork in the trunk. "I don't even have a ladder that high. It's amazing the fall didn't kill Oggy."

"Luckily, he has a lot of fluff to slow his fall."

As they walked the short distance back to the house to collect Oggy and the boys, Matthew asked, "Does your dad know about the baby yet?"

"Hmm. I don't know. Only if Jay told him." Robin sighed. "I guess I should call him." Dad's current wife, Sharon, was the worst to date. She was much younger than he, only a year or two older than Robin, and had three children of her own from two previous marriages. They were the three most obnoxious kids Robin had ever met. That and the fact that the woman was subtly hostile to her did not put talking to Dad high on Robin's list. "I could just text him. That way, I'm sure I won't have to talk to Miss PA."

"You shouldn't call her that." PA was Robin and Jay's pet name for Sharon, standing for passive-aggressive.

"It's a lot nicer than Jay's original nickname," said Robin.

"True. FB wasn't even accurate."

Robin made a face. "Stop. Just because you think she's hot gives you no right to defend her."

"She is pretty darn hot."

Robin punched him in the arm.

As they entered the house, Mason said, "He's just been sleeping, Mom. Do you think he's okay?"

"I think he's fine. He just needs to get back to his family."

"Family is important," said Matthew, catching Robin's eye.

She answered with a quick eye roll. Matthew was forever trying to rebuild bridges between her and Dad. But he wasn't the one who needed to do the construction. It wasn't like Dad ever went out of his way to call Robin or spend time with the grandkids.

"Come on," said Robin. "Let's get this little guy home."

Mason carried Oggy in a small cardboard box back to the edge of the woods. Once they grew near, Oggy began squawking with gusto. His parents answered. Within moments, the two adult owls winged silently from the canopy. They descended branch by branch. Once close, they began to fly in small circles. At first, they kept their distance, but as the four of them got closer, so did the parents. The wings of the male owl came so close to Robin that she could feel the slight breeze they made.

"Wow," said Mason. "They're kinda scary."

Matthew took Oggy from the box and stepped up to the base of the tree. He placed Oggy in the crate as quickly and as gently as he could. But he couldn't get away quite fast enough. Mama Owl swooped down, dragging her talons through his hair. Matthew screamed, dipped his head, and ran from the tree. Mason joined in with a scream of his own, while Ethan thought it was hilarious.

"Oh, you think that's funny, do you?"

Matthew swept up Ethan, and the four of them—heads down, arms up protectively—hightailed it out of there.

*A*uthor Note: Earlier, I mentioned that none of the bird names have been changed to protect the innocent. Oggy is the exception. If my brother named the little barred owl he kidnapped in the woods of South Carolina, he doesn't recall. The TV show Oggy and the Cockroaches first came out in 1998, so it is possible his name was Oggy.

Chapter 27: Breathe. Just Breathe.

The boys ran up ahead, all six of them screaming at the top of their lungs.

"Those owls are going to pluck out your eyes if you don't quiet down," Jay said more loudly than was probably necessary for the boys to hear him.

The day was hot and humid, making Robin feel like she was wading through a swamp. Gnats repeatedly attempted to land on her eyelashes, as if each lash was a diving board to the only cool pool in town. Jay slapped at some sort of bug. Robin brushed nearly frantically at her eyes. The buzzing of insects, the wetness of the air, and the noise of the boys were overwhelming.

Jay's youngest son picked up a rock and launched it toward his brother's head.

"Cut it out!" said Jay. He shook his head. "I should have been snipped at number three, but no, Christina just had to try one more time for a little girl. Never again."

Robin jumped at the chance to push away the buzzing. "Speaking of kids, I talked to Wren last week. Little Rain is giving her all kinds of grief."

"That's a baby for you," said Jay as he wiped away a dead bug smear and blood from his arm. It must have been a mosquito he'd slapped.

"I told Wren to bring Rain home and that you and Christina would gladly be her primary caregiver."

"Hilarious."

When Robin and Jay reached the tree, the boys were already standing on a log and taking turns peeking in at Oggy. The young owl hooted and stretched his neck over the top of the box. He'd grown so big in just a few short weeks. It wouldn't be long before he'd join his parents and his sibling. Only last week, she and Matthew had spotted the second baby owl peeking from the original nest cavity. Before long, the entire family would be together once again, up in the trees.

"Gross!" said Trevor, Jay's oldest.

Mason pushed Trevor from the log and climbed up. He reached in the box and pulled out a headless mouse. It dangled from between his thumb and forefinger. He hopped off the log and chased the younger boys. Several headless animals littered the ground. Trevor grabbed the nearest body and joined the chase. Within moments, it became a free-for-all, headless animals gliding through the air, peals of laughter, boys hitting the ground, and pine straw and dirt flying.

Robin just sighed. It was a good thing Oggy's parents had become accustomed to their frequent visits.

"They sure do bring him an abundance of food. And the offerings are always headless?" asked Jay.

"Always. They know it makes digestion and pellet production easier for the little guy."

"I certainly wouldn't want to poop out a head."

Robin smiled. It felt good to smile. "They regurgitate the pellet. You know, after indigestible things like claws, teeth, and skulls get compacted in the gizzard."

"Remember Grandma Elma? Now, her fried gizzards were to die for."

Robin couldn't help herself; she gave Jay a quick hug. He stiffened for a millisecond before relaxing and returning the hug.

"What's up?" he asked.

"I'm just affectionate. What can I say?"

He pulled away from her and gave her a hard look. "No, really. What's up?"

Robin tried to stop it, but her eyes filled with tears.

"Tell me," he said.

She leaned close so that only Jay would hear—although it was not necessary, with the ruckus the boys were making and the fact that they obviously weren't listening. Still, she brought her lips nearly to Jay's ear. "It's Matthew," she said. She had to step back and take a deep, calming breath.

Jay squeezed her arm, and she knew he was thinking she was going to say Matthew was having an affair. How she wished he were having an affair.

"It's medical. He doesn't want anyone to know."

She watched Jay's face drop from boys-will-be-boys commiseration to surprise and then to fear.

She leaned forward, her face near his. "Prostate cancer. We just got the biopsy report yesterday. The absolute worst. Small-cell neuroendocrine." She had to stop. She was going to lose it.

"Oh my God."

"He'd kill me if he knew I'd told you." She had to put out a hand and steady herself on Jay's shoulder. "I can't do it alone. I can't carry this around. Alone."

One of Oggy's parents hooted from above. Jay pulled her in to a place she never wanted to leave. She pressed her face against his chest.

Breathe. Just breathe.

Robin and Matthew walked slowly through the woods. Jay and Christina were watching the boys, giving them a rare evening alone. The sun was setting quickly, and at the pace Matthew was going, they would be lucky to get to the tree before all the light had disappeared. Robin removed her arm from Matthew's for just a second and pulled her sweater tighter around her. She wished she'd worn a coat. Matthew teetered, so she quickly reestablished her hold on him.

"Are you warm enough?" she asked.

He nodded. He was cold all the time. He was wearing his down winter jacket, a hat, and a scarf, even though it was only September and in the mid-fifties. She could feel him shiver.

"We won't stay long."

"I'm fine."

She sighed internally and willed herself patience. She wanted to shout, *If you say you're fine one more time, I will fucking kill you.* Which was such a horrible thing to think that it almost made her laugh.

"Look at the moon" was what she said instead. "I always love it when the moon rises at the same time the sun sets."

He didn't seem to know what she was talking about, so she stopped and pointed. "See it? Right through those branches? I think it's full tonight."

He nodded without really looking. She squeezed his arm, and he told her, "I like it when the moon rises with the sunset too."

She stood on her toes and kissed his neck.

When they finally reached the trunk, she held his hand as they scanned the branches of the nearby trees. They hadn't seen any of the owls for quite a while, but sometimes, when things were quiet, their faint calls could be heard.

"They're up there somewhere," she whispered. "I can feel them watching."

He tightened his grip on her hand. "There," he said.

Robin followed his finger to where he was pointing. She shifted so that she was more in his line of sight. Just when she was feeling she'd miss them in the fading light, there was a small movement in the branches. Two sets of young owl eyes glowed in the last rays of the setting sun. Like four full moons, they watched from the treetops. Robin and Matthew barely breathed as they looked back. And when it became too dark to see the owl moon eyes, the two of them walked slowly and carefully through the darkening forest toward home.

*A*uthor Note: *Barred owls mate for life and can live for over twenty years. They produce one clutch per season of two to four eggs, using the same nest cavity year after year. With beaks and claws, the young crawl out of the cavity before they can fly and hang out in the branches until their flight feathers have fully developed. Barred owls stay with their young much longer than other types of owls, forming a tight family unit that lasts through fall. Even when the babies are fully fledged, they tend to settle close by.*

Chapter 28: Aching with Life

Robin had to use the tip of her cane to unhook the hummingbird feeder from where it hung. She could no longer reach it—she'd shrunk that much in just a few short years. She made a mental note to ask Mason to lower it. Once the feeder's handle was on the cane, it slid down, banging her hand, cutting her thin skin, and spilling the little bit of residual sugar water on her hand and legs. Now she was bloody, sticky, and sweet. If she stumbled in the yard, she'd be consumed by ants before anyone would find her. The thought of this made her smile.

She licked at her wound before filling the feeder with fresh nectar. She stood on her toes, using one hand to steady herself with the cane while the other grasped the bottom of the feeder, and tried to reattach the wire handle to the hook. By the time she was successful, she was even stickier and sweeter. Luckily, her ability to clot was still intact—her wound had stopped bleeding.

Exhausted from her efforts, she made her way to the closest garden chair and sat down with a sigh. Let the ants take her away. There was nothing good and nothing noble about being so old. Ninety-four next month, she was hoping her gift would be a quick trip to heaven.

Almost immediately, two broad-billed hummingbirds descended on the feeder. She watched their blue iridescent heads and blur of wings with the same wonder she always had. The wind scooted over the courtyard wall and made her shiver, bringing with it the lovely scent of jasmine. She closed her eyes and listened to the many birds that filled her little courtyard. It was still desert-morning cold, the sun rising quickly. Soon, it would be warm enough for her to shed her jacket and then hot to the point she'd retreat to the coolness of the townhouse. She'd been in southern Arizona for more than twenty years and continued to marvel at the weather.

Morning in the desert, even when it was cold, was Robin's favorite time of day. She loved watching and hearing the birds wake up. Early spring, as it was now, was her favorite season. She might have been old, and it might have been thirty years since she'd had sex, but birds flitting around, their wings fluttering in a frenzy of passion, still turned her on.

Her cell phone chirped. Only her grandson MJ would be texting this early. With his new job at the Tucson post office, like her, he was up with the dawn. She tilted the screen to read it in the rising sunlight. Just as she'd thought, MJ had texted: *What up? I'm stopping by on my way to work.*

She struggled with the tiny keypad and gave him a thumbs-up emoji. Someone or other was always stopping by.

She'd never imagined herself leaving central New York. When Matthew died so young, leaving her with two young boys, at first she'd been too busy to think about where she lived. As the years wore on and her boys left the nest, she grew weary of the cold and snow. The dreary days weighed on her. Mason moved out west, and Ethan moved to Florida. She was alone except for Jay and his family, Mom having died twelve years after Matthew and Dad two years later. Wren and Rain were somehow lost to them, having not been heard from since soon after Matthew's funeral.

Ethan, having fully embraced palm trees, singles bars, and bachelorhood, never had any children. Once Mason and his wife started having babies, it was an easy decision.

"Come west, Mom. Your grandkids miss you. Sunny nearly every day. There are so many birds. Birds that I bet you don't even know about. And we need you."

He was wrong about her knowledge of the birds. She'd spent hours of her lonely nights researching bird species from all over the world.

But he was right about the sun, the joy her four grandchildren gave her, and the abundance of birds.

She regularly welcomed to her courtyard six species of hummingbirds—Anna's being her favorite—along with curve-billed thrashers, house finches, cactus wrens, dazzling vermilion flycatchers, and stunning phainopepla. She was entertained by the greater roadrunners running along the concrete wall of her courtyard. Gambel's quail nested in her potted plants. She watched Cooper's and short-tailed hawks circle above. She was frequently startled by the impressive and loud wings of ravens swooping in for a look. She smiled at the loud cackle of the Gila woodpecker every day and was lulled to sleep nightly by the hoot of great horned owls. She was even visited by an elf owl once, cocking his tiny head her way from the branches of the large mesquite that hung over her wall.

A rufous hummingbird buzzed above her head, apparently angered by having to share the feeder. He landed on a branch of a small desert willow and preened.

"Morning, Grandma," said MJ, sliding open the patio door and stepping into the courtyard. He placed a light kiss on her cheek and smiled. "You left your door unlocked again."

"I knew you were coming."

"No, you didn't. And you know I have a key. You really should keep your doors locked."

"What do I have that anyone wants?"

He shook his head and gestured surrender. It was an argument they'd had many times. Robin had no idea why he persisted.

"I need that hummingbird feeder lowered," she said.

"I can fill it for you."

"I like doing it. I was going to ask your dad to do it, but maybe you could."

"Sure thing. Next week."

"The birds empty it daily. I can ask your dad. I think he might stop by tonight."

MJ glanced at the time on his phone. "Do you have wire or a chain?" he asked impatiently.

Robin sighed. "Lowering it once will take less time than filling it every time you come." She sighed again. Years ago, she'd promised herself that she would never be a grumpy old lady. Here she was feeling very grumpy and very old.

"Do you have a chain or wire?" he asked again.

"Top drawer, to the right of the fridge."

He disappeared into the apartment. It was so hard to be a burden. It wasn't like she had any choice. Every night, she went to sleep, thanking the good Lord or the universe or whatever for giving her such a good life and wondering—even hoping—that she'd fall asleep and never wake up. But every morning, she opened her eyes and felt every part of her body ache with life. She was ready—more than ready—to join Matthew, who'd left her so long ago, or be rebirthed into her next life or burn in hell for that one wild affair she'd had with the married man five years after Matthew died.

She had never been steadfast in a belief of what happened after death. Having given it hours and hours of thought, she was no further ahead in her task of figuring the whole thing out. But the closer she got to finding out, the calmer she became. And maybe that was the secret of dying with grace and gratitude—just remaining calm. Steadfast calm.

A rustling in the corner of the courtyard caught her attention. An odd-looking curve-billed thrasher hopped into view just as MJ returned from the kitchen.

"Do you see that thrasher?" she asked.

"The what?"

"That bird. Over there by the bird bath." She pointed.

He looked at his phone rather than where she was pointing. "There are birds everywhere," he said, the impatience still in his voice. He stepped up to the hummingbird feeder, adding several links of chain. "Is that good?"

Even though it still looked too high, she smiled up at him. "Thank you, MJ. It's perfect."

He checked his phone again, tapping at the screen. "I gotta get going. I'll see you Monday, okay? I'm off to Sedona for the weekend."

"With a girl, no doubt."

He smiled. "No doubt." He kissed her cheek so lightly that it tickled. "Love you, Grandma." Before she had much of a chance to respond, he was gone.

She watched the hummingbird feeder swing from its new lower position. It didn't take long for the first of the birds to brave the moving target. Two more dropped into sight. "Glad he's gone," they seemed to hum. Robin settled into her chair and considered closing her eyes for a little bit. Before she had the chance, the odd-looking thrasher jumped again, closer this time. She could see that he was injured. Badly injured.

"MJ," she called. She considered texting him, requesting he return, but thought better of it.

Robin struggled to her feet and shuffled toward the bird. His neck was clearly distorted, a large hump forcing his head in a downward position.

"You look like Quasimodo," Robyn told him. "Poor thing. You must have flown into the glass."

The bird responded by trying to fly and failing. He landed hard and hopped away. He disappeared into the safety of a small staghorn cholla—a plant so covered in painful cactus barbs that even MJ could not have extracted him.

Robin teetered on her cane. She sighed. There was nothing to be done. Things lived, and things died. Very little of it—or none of it at all—was under her control.

Author Note: I promised at the beginning of Early Bird *that all my bird stories were based on true-life experiences. Staying true to that promise means that this story is reaching its conclusion. I'm just about out of bird stories! Maybe if I live as long as Robin, I will add to my list of re-markable bird encounters, but Robin's story has just one more episode.*

Chapter 29: What Every Death Deserves

Each morning, as Robin sipped her coffee and woke up with the birds, she searched for Quasimodo. Each morning, she was rewarded by his presence when he hopped out of the cholla, sometimes giving his wings a try. He grew stronger but was still unable to fly.

"You can live in my courtyard," she told him. "I know it's not the same. But you are alive."

Her granddaughter Sarah, Mason's oldest, came by with the great-grandchildren. They found the little hunchback fascinating and nearly irresistible. It was all Robin could do to keep them from chasing poor crippled Quasi.

Each time he'd disappear into the cholla, Benjamin, who was only two and a half, would ask, "Where he? Where funny-looking bird?"

Then he'd laugh and add, "He go in ouchy. That where."

Even MJ was interested. "How's Quasimodo?" he asked on those mornings he stopped by. He snapped photos, claiming he was going to post them on something called AmazoGram.

One evening, as the sun was nearly set, Robin and Mason shared a spicy burrito in the garden.

"He's still hanging in there," observed Mason. It was five days after his injury.

"I saw his mate a few days ago," said Robin. "She joined him on the ground. And hopped for a bit with her disabled partner. She even offered him bugs from her beak and nuzzled his neck."

"Really?" asked Mason.

"Uh-huh. And every once in a while, she'd fly to the top of the wall and call to him, like she was encouraging him to try to get over the wall. She eventually flew away."

"That's sweet and sad."

"I haven't seen her since." Robin shrugged. "Guess she gave up on him."

"Even sadder."

"I'm sorry, Quasi," Robin called toward the garden. "Not everyone can be a caretaker."

She turned to Mason and saw the last bit of sunshine on his face. "Every day, he grows stronger. I'm starting to have a little hope. It's really amazing that even the most crippled of creatures can find a place in the world. The will to live—you know, survival. It's quite an amazing thing."

As the days went on, Quasi got to the point that he could hop as fast as any robin she'd ever seen in New York. He easily snapped up bugs and drank water from the shallow dish she'd provided. He never let her approach him, but still, Robin fantasized that he'd grow so accustomed to her that she would someday stroke his hunched back and fully assess his injury.

"We're in this together," she told him.

Then one morning, she didn't see him. When it got too hot, she was forced inside, where she watched her shows, napped, and nibbled on the leftovers from the spaghetti dinner Mason's wife had brought her. She sat at her kitchen table, squinting out the window facing the garden, but Quasimodo never hopped by.

Once the sun dropped in the sky and the desert became habitable, she put on her sunbonnet and retrieved her cane. Slowly, she made her way through the potted plants and small scrubs of the courtyard. "Quasimodo," she called as if he were a dog. "Quasi?"

Finally, near the back wall, she found him, sitting in a ruffled heap. His head was tilted in a more exaggerated way. She bent down as far as she dared. Quasimodo had fresh blood on the side of his neck. She could just make out his spine sticking through his skin.

"Oh, what did you do, Quasi? Did you try to fly and reinjure yourself?"

He blinked and struggled to move away from her.

"Oh, Quasi. My poor Quasi, I will leave you to it."

Robin made her way slowly and carefully back to her apartment. She sat at her kitchen table a long time, watching the light grow soft in the courtyard, the shadows stretching, the birds' calls fading with the day. When it became fully dark, she prepared herself for bed, and when she was finally under the covers, she closed her eyes and knew that she would find her Quasi pretty much consumed by ants in the morning.

Robin sighed and snuggled deeper into the covers. She fell asleep looking forward to waking up. She fell asleep looking forward to her morning coffee with the birds. She counted on the fact that MJ would come tomorrow morning on his way to work. And although she knew he would do it grudgingly, she was quite certain that he would help her bury whatever was left of the bird. MJ would help her make certain that little Quasimodo's life was given the respect and the admiration that every death—and every life—deserved.

*A*uthor Note: *I hope you enjoyed* Early Bird, *and thank you for reading.*

About the Author

Karen Winters Schwartz wrote her first truly good story at age seven. Forty-five years later, her professional writing career finally began in 2010 with the first of five widely praised novels.

Educated at Ohio State University, Karen moved to the Central New York Finger Lakes region with her husband, where they raised two daughters and shared a career in optometry. She now splits her time between Arizona, a small village in Belize, and traveling the earth in search of the many creatures with whom she has the honor of sharing this world.

Read more at www.karenwintersschwartz.com.

About the Publisher

Dear Reader,

We hope you enjoyed this book. Please consider leaving a review on your favorite book site.

Visit https://RedAdeptPublishing.com to see our entire catalogue.

Check out our app for short stories, articles, and interviews. You'll also be notified of future releases and special sales.